Of Memory and Desire

Of Memory and Desire

Stories by
GLADYS SWAN

LOUISIANA STATE UNIVERSITY PRESS
Baton Rouge and London
1989

Designer: Sylvia Malik Loftin
Typeface: Trump Mediaeval
Typesetter: The Composing Room of Michigan, Inc.
Printer: Thomson-Shore, Inc.
Binder: John H. Dekker & Sons, Inc.

First Printing
98 97 96 95 94 93 92 91 90 89   5 4 3 2 1

Grateful acknowledgment is made to the editors of the following
publications, in which the stories in this book originally
appeared: *Greensboro Review* (Winter, 1980–81), "On the Eve of
the Next Revolution"; *Mid-American Review* (Fall, 1983),
"Getting an Education"; *New America* (Winter, 1980), "Land of
Promise"; *New Letters* (Fall, 1986), "July"; *Ohio Review* (1987),
"Lucinda"; *Sewanee Review* (Fall, 1981; Spring, 1983; Summer,
1984; Winter, 1986), "Reunion," "The Ink Feather," "Carnival for
the Gods," "Sirens and Voices"; *Writers' Forum* (1985, 1986),
"Black Hole," "Of Memory and Desire."

Library of Congress Cataloging-in-Publication Data

Swan, Gladys, 1934–
    Of memory and desire : stories / by Gladys Swan.
        p.   cm.
    ISBN 0-8071-1480-4 (alk. paper)
    I. Title.
PS3569.W247034   1989
813'.54—dc19   88-38353
                                                         CIP

À Monique,
Amie de mon enfance

It is always somewhere in the stirrings
of memory
that desire is born.

—Stendahl

CONTENTS

Acknowledgments

The author wishes to express her thanks to Alex Blackburn for his help and generous encouragement; to Thomas E. Kennedy for his efforts on her behalf; to the faculty and students of the Vermont College MFA Program for their continued support; and to Richard Swan for invaluable help with the manuscript.

Of Memory and Desire

Carnival for the Gods

It was the first time Dusty had ever backhanded her, and it was not just the blow, the pain, the blood from her lip flowing saltily into her mouth that gave Alta the shock: it was the sense that something fatal had struck at the roots of her life. Things would never be the same. It was the edge of Dusty's ring that had cut her lip, a gold ring with a strange little head carved in ivory that he'd bought during a fit of extravagance in Kansas City and said was his good luck and that he'd never part with it. As she stood in the cramped little bathroom, looking into the mirror, teeth all outlined in red as though she'd been eating red-hearted plums or pomegranates, the lip still bleeding, it seemed as though she'd never staunch the flow. This is my life, she thought; this is time leaking away, as it has been doing year upon year. And I'm standing here letting it happen like I was born without a brain.

The whole of the little trailer had shaken with their quarrel, till even words and the clash of voices could not contain the violence. Pansy, the little curly-haired dog she kept, a cross between a poodle and a wire-haired terrier, had taken refuge under the couch, and, looking at Alta with brown eyes that seemed full of the light of tragedy, still refused to come out. Dusty meanwhile had thrown himself out of the trailer and into the truck, banging doors all the way, setting up a cloud of dust as he roared off into town, leaving her there alone with the freaks and the animals in the broken-down carnival.

She dabbed at her lip as she tried to calm her feelings. She was looking pretty terrible at the moment. Face blotched, bags under her eyes, broken lip, but she wasn't all that old—forty-seven—and there was still a chance for . . . what? For love, for money?

Money talks—she'd learned that much. It says *yes* and it says *no.* Says, *you owe it to yourself, baby; go on and have it—be my guest.* Says, *you're out of luck, sister.* Says, *go to the city and have yourself a ball; says, stay home and starve your gut.* Says, *turn on the gold-plated faucet, break out the champagne.* Says, *stay away, lady, you smell bad, and nobody's gonna give you a second look.* Says, *dream—the sky's the limit.* Says, *look at the walls peeling.* Says, *go hang yourself.*

It says, Alta concluded, *you have been with a man who's brought you nothing but trouble and grief, all the while promising you the world.* And where has it landed you? Down in the flatlands with blood on your teeth. Always full of harebrained schemes. And he wasn't half as crazy as the rest of the outfit, only more unreliable.

"I'm sick of this life. Filled up to here." That's how it had begun.

Dusty, sitting at the narrow formica-topped table with the bench on either side, at which they had shared what might be called their domestic life, was adding up one of his interminable columns of figures. Always trying to turn nothing into something, as Alta had it, to make less come out to be more. "Sick of it."

He looked up. "There's no anchor hanging out of your ass."

The truth of this observation left her momentarily speechless—a yawl in a dead wind. Then her fury unlidded, and the fine brew the years had whipped to froth came boiling over, pouring out: the salt was in her mouth, the distillation of years of sweat and tears and gall. All she might have had—all that had gone down the drain.

It was the sandstorm that finally did it to her. Bad enough to have the equipment truck break down in the flattest, most god-forsaken stretch of natural freakishness she'd ever laid eyes on. Like somebody's uninteresting nightmare. A world created out of what any sensible being would've rejected in the first place or else reached for only in the dry heaves of violent boredom: things twisted and sharp and spiny and hard. Some of them reached up and out with arms dried and dead in their attitudes of empty aspiration. They seemed neither plant nor tree, these cacti and joshua trees; nor alive, these clutches of dry grass and sagebrush against a rocky ground that gave off a hard glint. The rocks that rose in the distance looked to have no living thing growing on them. Only telephone poles and the blacktop to show that human beings had been here—mainly, Alta thought, to get through it and on to somewhere else. The sort of place you might consider beautiful only if you didn't have to be there.

It was one of those undistinguished spots of blacktop, miles from the notion of a town, they'd come to a halt in the middle of, when the rear axle of the equipment truck broke down and their little procession came to an uneven halt, like train cars piling up. There was a dull, angry look in the sky, and they'd no sooner got their vehicles pulled off onto the shoulder than the wind picked up the dust and flung it at them, striking the metal roofs and sides like a flail. It was a good thing they weren't going anywhere, because they couldn't have seen to get there anyway. The sun was eclipsed, the windows dark with dust. And though the doors and windows were shut, so they were nearly stifled inside, the dust sifted through anyway, leaving a fine layer over everything. They drank it in their coffee and ate it with their food.

The animals nearly went crazy. The horses neighed and tried to rear in their trailer. The little elephant stamped and trumpeted. The tiger paced her cage all night. And what with the fray and the clatter, the bay gelding had somehow injured a leg. They needed both a vet and a mechanic—two more bills to pay. So it was no wonder that on this day, in what appeared to be the wreckage of the storm, most of the people in the show pulled out. The operators of the booths—little independent outfits that had hooked with them and would hook on somewhere else. The shooting gallery left and the lucky spinning wheel, the car races, the coin- and ring-tossing set-ups—most of the acts and all the games of chance were taking their chances elsewhere.

"Well, you gotta live," Pearl Diamond said when she and Bates, who threw knives at her till her silhouette stood outlined upon the wall and she stepped forth unscathed, were taking off. "Be seeing you," they said to Alta. "No hard feelings." The first to leave, they had put the idea into the common mind, though no doubt somebody else would have thought of it, too. Any woman, Alta thought, who trusted a man enough to allow him to throw knives at her was either too dumb or too lucky to have troubles in the world, and she envied her even as she wished her well.

If they hadn't missed the turnoff, probably none of this would have happened. They were supposed to have headed north toward Albuquerque, but they'd missed the sign and hadn't had the sense God gave a turnip to stop and look at a map. Before they knew it, they'd gone fifty miles out of their way.

If you hadn't . . . And how are we going to get out of this god-forsaken place? Money and blame. *Bitch, bitch, bitch. As if a man hasn't got enough troubles . . . Whose idea was it to . . . ? As if you never made a mistake . . .* Money and blame. *I could've made fifty to your one, and we'd both be better off.* Brickbats flying back and forth. *Pulling your weight . . . Whose weight? . . . Fed up with your . . . Because of you, goddamit. You gave me nothing, not even a child . . . Couldn't plant anything in that belly of yours except a fart . . . I should've got me a better man to try.*

The blood had dried on her lip. Tentatively she touched the spot, then turned from the mirror. *I could've been . . .* Not been—was. *Was* one of the best damn trapeze artists in the business. The two of them together: Gold Dust and Dream Girl. The dream had turned to dust—hah! Ashes to ashes: Gold Dust to Dusty, what a joke. The two of them one great act, till the moment suddenly came, maybe by a slip of the foot and one miss in midair too many, by too dizzying a glance down below, Dusty seemed to lose his nerve, wanted to settle for a life on the ground, but with higher ambitions: a show of his own. At the time when they could've had top billing in "The Greatest Show on Earth," Dusty chased his dream of something grander yet, circus and carnival together, triumphantly called "The Carnival for the Gods." Earth wasn't enough for him.

He was headed into the clouds, into the skyscape of the forever possible, the shape of things to come. They'd play all the big cities, bringing back the days when everybody went to the circus. Giant celebrations in the heart of every city.

But the idea never really got off the ground. It was too vast for anybody but Dusty to believe in for very long. The force of his enthusiasm—he could talk people into anything and they would follow him around with puppylike loyalty—held them for awhile. But starvation was a powerful eye-opener. The shine wore off, and off they went. And now they were down to the rag, taggle, and bob that had stayed because they had nowhere else to go.

There had been better days: when she was up on the high wire, and her body was a flash of motion as she swung, hanging by her heels, across the top of the tent, the faces below like rows of lightbulbs, her body light as a firefly in her blue body suit. All alone up there, no nets below, with the tight thrill that was the joy bred of danger. The tingle in the blood. God, how she loved it! It was the years that had brought her down to earth. She'd nearly killed herself once in a fall. She'd lost her timing, her body had gotten heavy despite all her efforts. The pull of gravity, the reluctance of the flesh. And all the while Dusty trying to put together his misbegotten scheme.

She put some water in the kettle to boil and took out a jar of Sanka. She didn't like the taste much, but even with the heat it was something to put into your mouth and swallow. Something to look into and stir your spoon around in while you sat. She spooned out the instant, poured in the water and sat ruminating, waiting for the coffee to cool, gazing into the dark liquid. Time out. It allowed you to sit down right in the midst of life while somewhere else people were killing each other or having babies or getting the mortgage foreclosed or carrying on a family quarrel that would leave seven people sworn enemies for life. But set a cup of coffee in front of you and none of it mattered, at least for the moment; otherwise, you were out scratching and biting and clawing because the world was an obstacle you had to strike out at.

She was full of yearning, but she didn't know what for. When she had had money, she bought clothes, strange fanciful outfits that could have taken her to another age and fashion, or to a costume party. She loved bodices decorated with pearls and sequins and fringes that shimmied when you walked and rhinestones that danced in the light. She loved bright colors: reds that could have come from the throat of a trumpet, and pinks and oranges and purples that peeled your eyeball back to the optic nerve. She had trousers and a turban made of cloth of gold, and tops all embroidered. Even now, when she took tickets she sometimes dressed up as the Queen of Sheba or a priestess of the moon in a gown, her special creation, that shimmered between gold and silver, set off by a crown of rhinestones with a fan of feathers rising from the back. But nobody paid any special attention. She had the stuff all packed in the closet. And Dusty wanted her to get rid of all that rubbish just taking up space, but it would have been like stripping off her own skin. Yet she knew she'd never wear them anymore. Most of them were too tight anyway.

No, money wasn't good for anything. It was good to spend when you had it, but then you tossed aside what you had bought like so much junk. Dusty still had his ring—so much for the luck it had brought him.

As for love, that was even worse. Had she loved Dusty, she wondered, or had she just wanted a man who dreamed big, was headed for the clouds?

He couldn't even give her a child.

Small wonder he had time to put the makings in her belly, considering where his head always was: scheming and dreaming and adding up columns of figures and charting their course around the country and talking half the night away, too excited even to make love. And though there were ups as well as downs at the beginning, things now were headed in one direction only. It didn't seem to occur to him that they were all washed up. The gaggle of folks they'd picked up was the rout, the survivors who hadn't quite gone over the edge, not the glittering argosy he'd always had in mind. A man with a dream was a madman.

Love. Much worse than money. A giant and a midget who fought and were inseparable. An animal trainer who was convinced a woman lived inside his tiger, the only woman he'd ever wanted. Idly, she wondered if anybody had ever tried fucking a tiger. She'd heard about doing it with cows and sheep and dogs. Probably even with trees, provided you weren't so unlucky as to strike upon a beehive inside. For all of which, she thought, you'd have to be pretty damn desperate. But a tiger? Even if you could get one to stand still for it, there was something in the nature of a cat that ought to make you a bit leery. You couldn't put your dependence on them. But then the trainer, Sam, was nuts, too. Love was too much. It created bizarre obsessions. It was a form of drunkenness and self-abuse. They threatened you with blindness if you twiddled your own organs, or with impotence or insanity. But they should've been smarter than that. Love itself was blind and impotent, insane, and ate the heart away until it was white and leprous and scarred beyond all telling. Never trust it, she thought.

Every once in a while when she needed to feel a little pride in herself, she got dolled up and ran off to have an affair with a truck driver or salesman or drifter who was looking for a little diversion. Men she didn't count on seeing again and usually didn't—or, if she did, the interest had passed. She used to like the thrill in the blood of having a new man, but even that had got old. She didn't trust it anymore, no more than she trusted a greenback. No, neither love nor money had taken her anywhere—just left her here tasting her own blood.

She wanted vaguely to kill somebody, but there wasn't anybody handy and certainly nobody worth the trouble. If it wasn't love and it wasn't money . . . The blood was beating in her veins. It went on beating and beating. Blood, sweat, and tears—maybe *they* were real. She found the water running out of her eyes. Real as dirt. Till you were dirt, too. They'd discovered America, and what was it but dirt? She looked outside. The dust had blown off, and under the blaze of sun the land was cooking into a piece of burnt toast. Maybe she should go out and start digging, see if she could strike oil. Wouldn't that be a humdinger?

Or maybe she should pull herself together and get up and leave like everybody else. She and Dusty had fought and torn at each other, had driven and goaded and disappointed one another nearly as far as human things can go. And now he'd made her taste her own blood, and she was still here. And what if from now on he made a pleasure of beating on her? Or if she stood for it . . . ? It made no sense. And if she left . . . what would she do? Go wandering through the world, probably, only by herself, waitressing at some café or bar. Trying to cadge drinks and lure men home. Even now there'd be snickers behind her back, not to think of the future.

She got up from the table and gave herself to the task of fixing supper: cut up meat and fried it with sliced onions and put in the tomatoes and chili peppers and set the pot on the stove to cook. What with the mechanic and the vet costing an arm and a leg, it might be her crew's last good meal for a while. Every time you took somebody a car or a body it seemed they wanted you to set them up for life. She'd make a big pot of chili that would either tide them over for a couple of days or feed whoever happened to wander in. Once she'd done that, she washed her face and cleaned herself up a little. She was needing company. She'd see what Billy Bigelow was up to.

She could count on him. He'd been with them forever, first as electrician, carpenter, handyman, what-have-you, and now, after the defection of Carnaby the Great, he was featured as Bigelow the Magician. He could pull cards from out of people's pockets and from behind their ears and discover scarves where they hadn't been before. He had mastered appearance and disappearance and seemed to want to climb to ever-higher steps of illusion. Though sometimes he would simply take a pile of long thin balloons and blow them up, twist them into dogs and lions and elephants and kangaroos and send them sailing out into the crowd.

She found him sitting on the couch in his trailer reading a

Time magazine. Probably months or a year old, since Billy never bought one. But the dates never interested him, it never mattered to him when an event had occurred.

"Dream Girl," he said, "come on in." He was the only person who ever called her that, and it seemed to be the only image he'd ever had of her: up in the air on the high wire. If it were anybody else, she'd be convinced she was being made fun of.

"Been looking at some moon shots they got here. All crust and craters."

"My God, why don't you look out the window? Isn't that desolate enough for you? If you get up and go outside, you could be on part of the moon they haven't discovered yet. The lower part."

"You really think the moon looks like this?" he asked.

"If it don't, it's missed a bet." She'd come over to joke a bit with Billy, but the direction the conversation was taking her, making her think about where she was, only brought on her irritability. She wished Dusty would come back so she could throw something at him.

"You know what I think?" Billy said, taking off his glasses so he could see her more clearly. "I think they go out and take all those pictures and say it's the moon."

"Why'd they do a thing like that? Besides, you got all those rockets going up and men coming down in capsules and stuff."

"Oh, you could fake that," Billy said, with a snap of the fingers. "No trouble at all. Just take a picture, put it alongside another and say it's the moon."

"What on earth for?"

"Because you got to keep one step ahead of the public. You got to keep them wondering, always in suspense. Otherwise they'd get so bored and dull in their minds they'd turn back into tree frogs. There they'd be, rocking back and forth going mumbledyboo and their eyes would go crossed and their lips would droop and pretty soon they'd be squatting in clusters like fungus, just trying to keep the burner going so life wouldn't go out altogether."

"You got some imagination."

"No, I mean it. That's why you got to have carnivals. Probably they got a secret genius agency somewhere with people that do nothing all day and night but think things up, one leap ahead of the rest of us."

"But all you're talking about is plain lies."

"Of course. What other kind is there? Except some lies are plainer than others. People need them, couldn't get along without them. Think about what people have believed, beginning with the earth being flat. All you have to do is get it into their heads and then they swear it's true."

"But now look," she said. "Nobody really believes you find cards behind their ears."

"They'd like to. And if you could convince them you got some leetle secret, they'd believe that, too."

He was always playing these games with himself, and she loved the way he twisted everything around till you didn't know whether you were coming or going. She'd lost all her anger. "Well, if everything can be a lie," she said, "then everything can be true just as well." She hadn't the faintest idea what she meant.

"Because people believe it? Then anything can be the truth, can't it? Like all that stuff about living past lives. That could be true."

"Suppose it is. I can't say it isn't. I can't say people haven't been on the moon."

"The people from the future would be living right now, wouldn't they?"

"And how would you know?"

"Use your head. It's got to follow," he said. "And suppose you could go back to the past and you killed your grandfather, would you be alive now?"

"Of course not," she said offhandedly, even though she knew she was being had.

"But then how could you go back . . . ?"

"Why weren't you born with two heads?" she wanted to know. "Then one of you could live in the past and the other in the future and tell each other all about it."

"Probably fall flat on my face," he said, "and the present would go leaking through."

"Through the hole in your head." She stopped, all used up. "How come you don't leave like the rest?"

"The show must go on," he said.

"Come on," she said. "What show? This flea-bitten, half-assed . . . "

"I love you, Alta—you have such a high opinion of we serious professionals." She couldn't tell if he was teasing her or making fun of himself, or maybe both at once. "I'm a magician."

"And an electrician and a carpenter and—"

"A man of parts," he said.

"Is one of 'em a stomach?" she asked. "I've got chili cooking."

"Gotcha."

Back in the trailer she stirred the chili, added some oregano and cumin and then sat down to look at the copy of *Vogue* she'd slipped out of the dentist's office the time she had a toothache in Biloxi.

The sun had really turned on the juice so she tried to get a little relief by opening the window and turning on the fan. But the flies came in through a tear in the screen and buzzed around her head, and Pansy sat and snapped at them. Now and then she glanced out the window to watch Fred taking care of his horses. He'd taken them out of the trailer one by one and tethered them over by some scrub cedar. He'd brought out hay and water and then had lingered in the heat, grooming them, talking to them and trying to soothe them and make up for a life that offered no explanations, just endless travel, unexpected stops, dust storms, injury, and inconvenience—all for the sake of those few triumphant moments in the ring when Ginger, his wife, leapt and danced across their backs.

Every now and then a car or a truck would come whooshing past with a rush of hot air and a slash of light, then go plummeting on into the distance. She had no idea when Dusty would be back. Maybe he'd just taken off like the others. Then a truck—not his—appeared, slowed, and finally stopped across the road from the horse trailer. A lean, wiry man got out, took a leather bag from the seat, and walked over to where Fred was working with his horses. The vet. As she watched them, a couple of tow trucks pulled up and parked. A burly man, T-shirt sticking to his chest, sunglasses, got out. Then a tall guy, cap on his head, long arms, big hands. Burt, their equipment man, emerged from the rig and came over to talk to them. Then a lot of backing and maneuvering, hauling of chains and attachments. And after a time they were towing the truck away in the direction of what she supposed was a town, though more than likely nothing more than a mirage. She'd believe it when she saw it. But no Dusty.

Then the vet was gone, too, and she watched Fred lead the horses back into the trailer. That done, he walked over to the trailer where he lived with Ginger, who leapt from one horse to the other as they raced round the ring, who went up into a handstand or did a flip at the height of their motion, who was beautiful to watch. There was a lightness in her. They deserved better, Alta knew. They were young and, like everybody else who'd been drawn in, had the dream painted in their heads. All full of enthusiasm. Dusty's dream was their dream. She'd seen it happen over and over again. And he wasn't lying when he went on painting the sky in vivid colors. He believed every word of it: it was going to happen. Then, one day, they woke up. He owed them money, like he owed everybody money.

Now she knew they were leaving, too. She didn't get up to say goodbye, though she and Ginger had sat in each other's trailers and traded intimacies. And Ginger had showed her bruises on her body in places that didn't show. And sometimes she'd wept: Fred was fonder of his horses than he was of her, treated them better. And to tell the truth, she was sick of the smell of horse. Fred always smelled of horse. Alta didn't go over to say goodbye, because chances were they'd come across each other when they least expected it. In this business you were never surprised.

She felt bad about the money, but there was no help for it. If their paths did cross and Dusty were flush, he'd pay off. That's what he said, and she had no reason to doubt him because so far Dusty hadn't had any money. She watched Ginger climb into the cab of the trailer while Fred went back to drive the truck with the horse van. Then they were gone. Why wasn't she leaving with them? Was one kind of wandering any worse than another?

For a time she sat there blank and empty, all used up. The anger of the morning seemed as far away as last month. She wasn't even waiting for anything. She turned off the chili, then let the evening move in around her. She sat with her dog in her lap. The deepening sky was a rich blue, a mingling of blues, lighter and dark, with a smoky feeling underneath; it came down into the landscape, softening the edges of the mountains, turning brown slopes to lavender, to indigo, to darker shapes yet that made all part of one vast stillness that reached far beyond her, perhaps to the borders of the world. There were only the little lights of the few trailers left: animal trainer, giant and midget, magician-cum-handyman. That was the carnival now—the scrapings from the pot.

From out of the indigo she saw headlights approach, then heard a truck pull up and stop. She went outside. It was Dusty back, but with somebody beside him in the front seat. She bent down, leaning on the side of the truck to look in. A girl. She could just about make her out in the gathering dusk. Though she looked to be no more that seventeen-eighteen, she knew everything a woman could know and then some.

"This is Grace," Dusty said, by way of introduction. "Amazing Grace. Wait'll you see what she can do. We'll hit the big time yet."

I know what she can do, Alta thought. Amazing, all right. Probably one of those street kids that had left home at twelve or thirteen, soon as their periods started and they had their union card for womanhood. Then they peddled it on every street of Everytown in the great U.S. of A. Double A for Amazing. Then she noticed a childish face in the narrow seat behind Dusty. A boy. But so wild he looked like some creature

that had been torn away from the land and still carried in its
eyes the reflection of the water hole from which it drank, the
snug of the nest where it had spent the night still clinging to
the fine white hairs on his arms.

"Does he talk?" she suddenly asked.

"The words have gone out of him," the girl said, "but the
singing has stayed behind. He knows the Ballad of Kitty Mo-
reno and Amigo and the Battle of Glorieta Pass and Indian Joe
and his fight with a bear and the loves of Pajarito."

These are barely human things, Alta found herself thinking, for she had learned to recognize such and they were not
new to her experience. And here was another set in front of
her that she might look at and talk to and never understand.
She could ask questions till her teeth rotted and it wouldn't
make a ghost of a difference. There they were, almost cringing
in the seat of the truck. In the back with the boy, she noticed
two crates that looked to be the dimensions of their personal
property and inside which something stirred and moved with
a vaguely animal and somewhat sinister quality. She didn't
ask what.

"You want something to eat?" she asked, for she could
recognize hunger, too, though on what level she couldn't always tell. "I've got a pot of chili on the stove."

They stepped out of the truck then, the girl rubbing her
arms against the evening chill. Alta saw a square of light
as the door of Billy Bigelow's trailer opened. He'd be coming, too.

She looked off into the distance before she went inside:
over in the mountains it looked as though a storm was brew-
ing up. A sudden flash of lightning and the mountains stood
out, every slope and draw outlined in angular crossings of
brilliance. If it rains, she thought, it will pick up the dust and
the sky will fall down in mud. First they'd nearly been swept
away, now it was more than likely they'd be mired down. Or
else the water could come tearing down the mountains in a
flash flood.

"Come on inside," she said, and went to the stove to put the
fire on. Dusty was still fiddling outside in the truck while

these two stood uncertainly in the doorway. "You can wash up in there," she said. The boy's eyes went roaming around the trailer as if it would take getting used to. Alta went about setting the table.

Here they were, just another pair among the number she had seen, in the procession of all the broken, ill-formed, misbegotten things headed out of the world and onto the road, moving from town to town, never calling any place their own. They were her family, if you could call it that—they were her fate.

She closed the front door. It was getting cold now as night took over the desert. She was closing the door against the night, against the rustle of lizards and the spines of cactus, against whatever shapes lay in the darkness and whatever moved in the silence. Then Billy Bigelow and Dusty came in talking about the day. Only the sound of voices and the smell of chili seemed warm and real.

Getting an Education

Most of the neighbors took in the oddities of Findlay Brightwood the same way they took in everything else: the domestic quarrels of the Ryans; the untidy family life of Dr. Kiely—
Eye, Ear, Nose & Throat—whose wife let the kids run wild
with neglect; the heavy drinking of the Pattersons, who par-
tied lavishly on weekends, going through *her* money like
water, leaving out a full case of whiskey bottles for the garbage man to cart off the following Monday after their friends
had departed in drunken riot.

"Those kids are going to turn into juvenile delinquents,"
Crystal Munsinger heard her mother say often enough.
"They're driving me wild." Or: "Those people are drinking
themselves to death. I couldn't sleep last night for the noise."

But though the neighbors gossiped and judged and deplored
such behavior, they could not forget the social position of the
people involved. It was like discussing the follies of kings. All
in all, it made pretty good entertainment.

Finney Brightwood was a different case, however. His kind
of eccentricity seemed to come of having a head so crammed
full of knowledge he was helpless as a baby when it came to
the practical side of life and could barely live in the world. He
was a college professor newly hired to teach history at the
local teachers' college. He'd come all the way from California,
bringing his Ph.D. and his mother, a stenographer newly retired from the Los Angeles Police Department with a certifi-
cate of merit for thirty years of dedicated service.

Crystal watched him move in across the street, into the
modest little house that sat between the money of the Patter-

sons and the power of the Ryans, who figured heavily in local politics and owned half the town besides, including the great pink stuccoed adobe in which they quarreled. Mrs. Baynes lived on the other side of the Ryans. And though, as Mrs. Munsinger expressed it, she'd been no more than a salesclerk in the local department store and was homely as mud, she'd been married late in life to a man who'd made a fortune in the mines. Now as a rich widow she was therefore entitled to put on the dog and would speak only to the Ryans and the Pattersons.

Crystal's side of the street was a line of neat modest little houses like the one Dr. Brightwood was moving into. So that those who lived in them were able to look across to money and knowledge and power, in an unbroken vision from the Kielys' house on the corner, with the high fence around it to keep the neighbors out but not the children in, down to Mrs. Baynes's two-story mansion with the statue of Cupid in the yard, flanked by a swan. Though Clayton Thurgood, a telephone repairman, commented as the moving van drove off and left Dr. Brightwood in the midst, "All those college professors are either communist or crazy," not everyone agreed.

"He'll be a great asset to the neighborhood," Mrs. Munsinger insisted.

Crystal, her daughter, was the first member of the family to go to college, and the importance of an education had been impressed upon her ever since she could remember. For her mother, the title of doctor, lawyer, congressman called up an immediate awe; anyone who had a profession was a superior being. Education spelled opportunity. Crystal knew that her mother would be overjoyed to see money and social position come her way. But in any case, she wanted her to be a teacher so that she could be somebody in the world and not have people look down on her.

Crystal herself was full of uncertainty. In her sophomore year of high school she'd been transplanted to this remote corner of New Mexico from Lima, Ohio, where her father had sold insurance. The move was to alleviate her mother's asthma, but it had at the same time shattered what little social ease Crystal had managed to develop from her years of growing up in the same town and neighborhood. She had wept to leave behind the two or three friends she had, along with her school and her sense of place. Instead of trees and grass she found cactus and mesquite; miners and cowboys instead of salesmen and company employees—and through it all a nasty suspiciousness between Mexicans and Anglos, as they were called. Her only real friend during high school had been the college librarian, who chatted with her when she went to check out books. "She's always got her head buried in a book," her mother was fond of saying, to Crystal's embarrassment. Now she was starting college.

At eight o'clock on the first day of the fall semester, Crystal found herself in Dr. Brightwood's freshman social studies class in a large lecture room on the second floor of the main building. It was a required course, and the room was nearly full. Before the bell rang, Dr. Brightwood appeared. When he walked into the classroom, the girl behind her tittered. He was so short he was all but hidden by the lectern. What was worse, he had the most fantastically skewed eyesight Crystal had ever seen. She learned later that he had but one good eye. As he explained his attendance policy, which was fixed and harsh and fair, the one eye, nearly sightless and planetary, wandered off on its own, now looking up at the ceiling, now at the other side of the room, while the good eye, only slightly off-center, mostly looked ahead. He called roll.

"But you can't tell if he's looking at you or not," Crystal heard one of the girls say after class.

It was true. When he looked at a person, he was looking at two people, and sometimes two students answered from widely separate locations in the classroom.

But he can't help his eyes, Crystal thought, as she sat in the back of the room in an agony of embarrassment for him. To make sure that she was really the one being called upon, she always waited until he actually spoke her name. But several of the students seemed to enjoy the confusion. This trick of his eyesight seemed to leave Dr. Brightwood even more confused than his class and he would look round wonderingly as though he had suddenly found himself in a strange place.

Perhaps Crystal would have thought less about Dr. Brightwood had she seen him only four hours a week in the classroom when she was not fully awake anyway, but he was her neighbor as well. Now of a morning she found herself in his company on the way to school, and he led her at a breathless pace up the hill. Once, as they raced along, Dr. Brightwood explained between breaths that he was a runner, had run the mile at the University when they told him he'd have to take P.E. and had been running ever since. She quickly discovered that he could walk faster than she could run. At the top of the hill, he would take out his pocket watch and check his time. "Not bad," he would say with a certain triumph as she tried to catch her breath. He reminded her of the White Rabbit.

Crystal learned from her friend the librarian that people had been inviting Dr. Brightwood to dinner and that he'd been dropping hints that, being nearly forty, he was ready to get married and would be glad to meet a likely young woman. He had, in fact, spent most of an evening at the librarian's house gazing with his good eye at the picture of a dark-haired señorita romantically portrayed. The librarian had been amused.

It was a surprise to Crystal that Dr. Brightwood would think about women at all, though she could not say why. Nor could she imagine him standing with a dark-haired señorita by his side.

"But I think he'll not be marrying," the librarian said with a smile.

"Why not?" Crystal wanted to know.

"I think he's a congenital bachelor," she said.

Congenital. Congenital. Crystal went home and looked up the word to make sure. Were some people born to be bachelors and others not? She was mystified. It was like the pronouncing of one's fate. But the librarian could be wrong.

And everyone had been eagerly inviting him to dinner. But wherever he was invited, he always brought his mother, who

monopolized the conversation by talking about the achieve-
ments of her Findlay. "I think," the librarian said, "that after a
little while, people will stop inviting the new professor."

"Well, I'm on my own," Dr. Brightwood announced to
Crystal one morning during their race up the hill.

"And how is your mother?" Crystal asked politely, as she
had been taught to do, for his mother was in the hospital for a
week having a gallstone removed.

"Coming along nicely, but a little weak yet. It'll be a relief
to have her back," he said. "I'm getting tired of cornflakes."

"Cornflakes?" Crystal said, in a burst of surprise.

"That's all I've had to eat."

Nothing else. He didn't know how to cook anything, he
told her. "I don't even know how to use a can opener."

Crystal looked at him in wonder: his face was that of a
happy child. As he was telling her these things, he seemed
somehow delighted with himself.

Crystal was trying to be a student and to discover what she
ought to be learning. She felt not only ignorant but stupid,
and wanted to know what would make her smart and sure,
but though she studied hard and got straight A's, it didn't
seem to make any difference. She had the sense that she was
utterly in the dark. What she was missing or how to find out
seemed to escape her.

Dr. Brightwood taught history in a way that made it boring
and easy. He didn't lecture or discuss. He spent the class time
reading from the text sentences he expected the students to
learn by heart and write down word for word on his tests. One
always had to remember that certain events happened *about*
and not *on* a certain date, *circa* 1500, for instance, and that
certain statements required the provision of an *and/or* as part
of their testimony. If one left out a *circa* or an *and/or*, the
answer was marked wrong with a great red slash. But what
dictated the choice of information for the students to memorize was, for Crystal, a mystery without a clue. She had to
write down in her notebook that the Straits of Gibraltar were
named for Tariq Ibn Ziyad, the Berber chieftain who had
crossed them. Years later she was unable to forget that fact.

A trick of the students was to ask Dr. Brightwood for details of his personal history in order to divert him from giving them more "study suggestions" for his tests. These were far more interesting.

"Dr. Brightwood, tell us about the time when . . ." And he was led on while the class listened with suppressed mirth. He told the class how he came to be a runner and described the various stages of his Ph.D. But just when his history seemed to be exhausted by the only two things he had done in his life, he said one day:

"It's true that now I have to earn my living as a history professor and take care of my mother, but my real career has been as an explorer." His eye wandered around the classroom while a little thrill of interest traveled through it. "On my last expedition to Mexico I nearly lost my life. I went there to explore a cave with a great treasure hidden in it by the Aztecs, but it was under a curse . . ."

So, Crystal thought, he has had an adventure: so many lives seemed to get on without any. She felt a sudden respect.

At that point he paused, stood for a moment as though waiting for the reaction of the class, then dramatically left the room. A few minutes later the bell rang and the class left in a buzz without him.

As he and Crystal were climbing the hill together the next day, Dr. Brightwood explained his sudden departure.

"Do you know what happened to me?" he asked, with an expression she'd come to recognize. "My false teeth just locked right together and I couldn't say a word."

He told her this with the same sort of directness and amusement that came with his confession about living on cornflakes. It seemed to her that he could appreciate almost any sort of joke on himself. But she'd have died before she told such a thing to anybody. She couldn't bring herself to tell anyone in the class about Dr. Brightwood's false teeth. And it *was* funny.

One evening near midterm, Crystal, seized by a fit of restlessness, spent an hour wandering around the campus avoiding the library. She had walked up the hill from her house in time to see the last stragglers emerging from the dining hall. Most of the time she studied at home, and when she came back in the evening she was reminded that there was a life on the campus that she wasn't part of at all. She was met by a little knot of students, among them Judy Simpson, whom she knew only as a girl all the football players wanted to date—all the mean, rangy boys from West Texas. Each time Crystal saw her, she had a different one in tow. She wasn't even very pretty, Crystal thought, but rather bland, moon-faced. She never said a word in class, never knew any of the answers when she was called on. The girls envied her popularity. Once she'd said that all she wanted to do was get married. It seemed likely she would manage it before the year was out. As for herself, Crystal did not think she would ever marry.

It was a chill evening, not quite dark. The lights were on in the library and the dorms and in one of the classrooms in the main building. Crystal was in time to see the Farnison brothers, Lyle and Rennie, cross the campus carrying a hand organ between them that they were taking to Vespers, held every evening in the classroom now awaiting them. They were not like the fellows who lived in Enloe—a rowdy bunch who spent one Saturday night hurling empty beer cans at the dorm. Polite and clean and nice, they never dated and seemed determined to remain pious Christians despite all the corrupting influences around them. They would never do anything wrong, Crystal thought, not in their whole lives. She could tell even from the way they walked. She wondered what it would be like never to have to make mistakes.

She shouldn't be wasting her time, she knew, glancing at her watch. She had a paper due, a test to study for. Even so, she went over to The Cooler, where she found a group of girls from her class, notes laid out on the long table in back, in the midst of coffee cups and coke glasses. Crystal bought a cherry coke and sat down with them.

"And the Plantagenets," Glorietta Van Duyn mimicked, trying for Dr. Brightwood's walleyed look, "took their names from the *Planta genista* or broom plant." They all laughed.

It was not a very good imitation, really. But Glorietta was an actress and was going into the Theater, and everything she did was a performance. She never sat down, she draped herself into a chair, and all her gestures were larger than life. Crystal envied her, for she had gotten the lead in the fall production of *Camille*, in which she had languished so long and coughed so violently, it looked as though her first play might be her last. But to stand up on stage and do that . . . Crystal thought.

When she left the girls nearly an hour later, she could not claim to knowing more than when she had arrived. She would hardly have time to make a beginning. She walked quickly past the Art Building, where the lights were on and a solitary student was working in one of the rooms. Russell Snelgrove. She knew who he was—he was known all over campus, though he scarcely spoke a word to anyone. He claimed to be a full-blooded Apache Indian.

This conviction had asserted itself one morning at sunrise on a hill over by the edge of the married student housing. At least one couple was aroused in time to see a man in full Indian dress, complete with feathered warbonnet, doing a war dance and yelling in blood-curdling fashion. The rest of the time he walked about the campus in proud silence and took courses only in lapidary and jewelry making. He spent long hours polishing stones. He was a slender man with lily-white skin, and a distant look. The rumor reached Crystal that he wrote his own pornography and sat and read it at night with great relish. Crystal had never seen any pornography.

By the time she had climbed the hill where the library stood above the rest of the campus, the lights were beginning to go out. She had wasted the whole evening. She lingered a little while on the front steps, looking down at the lights of the dorms and the houses of the town that lay below. She was entirely at loose ends. She thought of the people she knew and didn't know. How was it that people's lives took a certain direction, that they were what they were? Things made a curious sort of twist as they came from the center of another person's meaning into her observation, and seemed to turn wild and fantastic. She didn't know what to think or how to be. There was just all this waiting for something different to happen.

She tried to imagine herself standing in front of a classroom. She saw herself moving her lips with no words coming out. Then laughter.

Dr. Brightwood kept putting off telling his class the finale of his expedition to Mexico. But finally he was badgered into it. Crystal had been wanting to ask him about it, but everybody had scoffed so much about his tale and made such fun of him she was afraid to take him seriously.

Alone—he told the class—despite the entreaties of his fellow explorers, he had gone into that dark and twisting cavern, lighting matches to find his way. (A snicker at the back of the classroom.) Then suddenly he knew he should not take another step. Lighting his last match, he saw that he stood at the edge of a deep chasm filled with water. There at the bottom lay the skulls of thousands of men. Then the match went out. How Dr. Brightwood found his way back and was happily reunited with his companions was unclear. On that day the class received no study suggestions.

"And how are things going in Dr. Brightwood's class?" the Dean, for whom Crystal worked as a typist, asked her not long afterwards.

"It's so dull," she found herself saying. "He makes us memorize all these facts. And they're not important . . ." She was astonished at herself.

After listening for a few minutes, the Dean said simply, "Dr. Brightwood is a gentleman and a scholar." The conversation was concluded.

For a moment, Crystal was almost ready to agree and to feel that she had located but one more area of her insufficiency. Yet when she looked at the various labels, *congenital bachelor, gentleman and scholar, oddball,* the figure of Dr. Brightwood became strangely obscured. What did he have to teach her? Perhaps when she reached that ideal toward which her education was to lead her, she would know: there would be instant enlightenment. But for the moment it seemed a questionable promise. Perhaps she might reach the precise point where fact and fancy could be separated, as neatly as Dr. Kiely's fence kept him separate from the neighbors. For the moment she couldn't even be sure which was which. And right now she was ready to throw away Tariq Ibn Ziyad and keep hold of the adventures in the cave in Mexico, perverse though such a choice might be. The tale, she knew, was pure fiction; Dr. Brightwood, a joke. Yet by a trick of the imagination she had accompanied him some distance on that perilous journey, had wanted to reach out and clutch him by the arm to prevent him from taking that fatal step. In an odd way, the tale, whether fact or fiction, belonged to him, like his watch or his morning race up the hill. It was like a fragment of glass, curious and bright-colored and in itself useless, that she had picked up to save, as she used to do as a child because it appealed to her imagination.

That spring Johnny Ryan gave Dr. Brightwood twenty-five strawberry plants, which he proceeded to plant upside down.

"Dr. Brightwood is such a wonderful son, so devoted to his mother," Mrs. Munsinger said in the tone she kept for reverence. She was sitting by the front room window, where both she and Crystal could observe the familiar sight of Dr. Brightwood giving his mother her daily exercise. The old woman walked in little baby steps, so that it took considerable time for her to reach the corner. It was as though Dr. Brightwood were teaching his mother to walk.

"She can walk perfectly well when he's not around," Jane Edwards had told Crystal. For now he hired college girls to come to clean and cook the meals for himself and his mother. "I take her down to the beauty shop once a week to get her hair done," Jane said. "And she pops out of that car as lively as a chicken. But the moment he's around, suddenly she's as helpless as a babe."

That year, Crystal's sophomore year, the newly hired psychology teacher conceived a passion for Dr. Brightwood. Every time he walked past her office on the first floor of Light Hall, she would try to waylay him in conversation or else she would call out to him, "Oh, Dr. Brightwood, hello. Hello, you cute little man."

He would blush like a schoolgirl. It seemed to Crystal that

he ran faster down the hall than she'd ever seen him run up the hill. And she thought of what her friend the librarian had said, of what Jane had said, and wondered why some people married and "popped out children like so many peas," as her mother put it, and why someone like Dr. Brightwood was still a son to his mother. It struck Crystal as curious that Dr. Brightwood wore both a belt and suspenders. He was the first person she'd ever known who wore suspenders.

"A wonderful man," Mrs. Munsinger was saying, with that clear and certain judgment she had for applying to the world's particularities and untwisting the skein of right and wrong. "Why, they're talking to Minna Patterson. She's gotten so snooty lately she wouldn't even say hello to me on the street the other day."

Here was, Crystal saw, but one more proof to her mother that it was intelligence that finally meant something in the world, let people say what they would. That was why she was so happy that Crystal was going to end up as a teacher.

But Crystal knew that she was still looking for a knowledge that continued to elude her. Everything lay coiled and indecisive, most of the time afraid to put forth the bud of an opinion. She drifted about in a boredom that was a kind of misery, while judgments flew all around her. But each time she picked one up, she found it only partly workable, endlessly qualified the closer it got to her experience, or else it dissolved like a snowflake.

For her mother, things worked out more simply. She moved things around like the pieces of a dime store puzzle. It all came together neatly as horses in a pasture, flowers in a garden. The pieces formed a picture and no riddle lurked beneath. If you followed the rules, things came out right. But if you drank too much or neglected your kids, they came out wrong. There was a picture but no puzzle. She just couldn't understand why people were so stupid.

Crystal, on the other hand, was always wondering what went on in people's minds. Her own seemed so murky that to find out what was in it was like letting down a hook in dark waters and waiting for one of the creatures that went swimming by.

She took up smoking and shocked everyone by walking into class one morning smoking a cigarette in a long black cigarette holder. She did not smoke at home, only at school. She got a *B* that spring in Dr. Brightwood's English history course because she cut four times. She still walked up the hill with him in the morning.

That summer Dr. Brightwood and his mother were gone from the neighborhood for a month. They went off for a vacation for the sake of his mother's health—to a dude ranch in Arizona. Crystal wondered what they were going to do at a dude ranch.

While they were gone, the neighbors noticed unusual activity in Dr. Brightwood's house: there were cars parked along the street in front, coming and going all night long. It appeared that Dr. Brightwood had left the key with the woman who was now coming in to clean for him. While he was gone, she made his home into a one-woman whorehouse. Johnny Ryan laughed about it, the way he laughed when "Old Finney" had put in the strawberry plants upside down. But Mrs. Munsinger was incensed; it was a disgrace to the neighborhood. Not that she blamed Dr. Brightwood. It was just that, as she explained to Crystal, the world was full of low types that couldn't be trusted.

In her junior year Crystal moved into the dormitory and, since she wasn't in any of his classes, she did not often see Dr. Brightwood. From that point on, she took mostly education courses, which she found more boring than anything she had taken so far. She had to memorize the Seven Cardinal Principles, which had to do with developing character and leadership and demonstrating the proper use of leisure time.

It was with dread that she looked forward to student-teaching during her senior year. Yet she managed to stand in front of her first class and teach the lesson despite the panic that threatened. Though she was sure that none of the students paid any attention, that they waited only for the hour to be over, she managed to keep some semblance of order in the class for a whole semester. She graduated with honors, much to the satisfaction of her parents, and even found a job teaching history and English in a junior high school in northern New Mexico.

But after a year she gave it up. She had no idea what to teach a Mexican kid who lived in a one-room dirt-floored adobe hut in the company of eight or nine brothers and sisters. She went to work for a newspaper but felt equally dissatisfied. Not long after, she married a young reporter she met on the staff.

She continued to receive letters from her mother about people in the neighborhood. Old Mrs. Brightwood was getting more and more feeble. The two of them, mother and son, seemed to be entirely alone—nobody came to visit. Sometimes, her mother wrote, she took over a piece of cake when she baked, and they were always very grateful. Minna Patterson had gone to a sanitarium for a rest cure—"to be dried out," as her mother put it. And Mrs. Baynes, always such a tightwad, was flinging away her money in Las Vegas.

It occurred to Crystal after reading one of her mother's letters that she'd been taking in such details all her life, fact and fancy, bits of craziness and wonder, things large and small, crooked and straight, superficial and devious, excessive and lacking—unable to discard any of it, but having to make space for it all: Tariq Ibn Ziyad and the Aztec cave, Russell Snelgrove and Mrs. Baynes and her own mother as well. It was like so many fragments of glass that the light shone through, first one way, then another. And each time you took out the collection to add another piece, you found that the light had shifted and nothing was the same.

And yet, Crystal thought, you might add the pieces, but perhaps through it all, curved like a snake or the bed of a river, something was being created, so that after a time you were looking at a strand, a connection, a pattern. For hadn't Minna Patterson been drinking too much ever since Crystal knew her?—though Crystal didn't know why. And wasn't Dr. Brightwood's life but a continuation of what had been?

So that she was not altogether surprised by what happened to Findlay Brightwood after his mother died. Mrs. Munsinger thought he might marry now that he was free of his responsibilities and still relatively young, just approaching fifty. And it was with shock and outrage that she discovered that Dr. Brightwood was having a series of affairs—with male lovers.

But then the neighborhood was going downhill, Mrs. Munsinger wrote. Johnny Ryan had shot himself after one of the violent quarrels between him and Bernice: Bernice had driven him to it, she was sure. And Dr. Kiely's youngest son had been hauled in for the second time on a drugs possession charge— she'd always known those kids would come to no good. And Minna Patterson was dying of cirrhosis of the liver. Mrs. Munsinger was ready to move out of the neighborhood and was thinking of selling the house to a Mexican woman who had the down-payment, let the neighbors think what they would.

No, Crystal thought, she was not surprised about Dr. Brightwood.

Then came the final piece of news. Findlay Brightwood was found dead in his living room, apparently the victim of foul play by one of his "boyfriends," as Mrs. Munsinger put it. The place was in frightful disorder, everything torn apart, though there was no reason to suspect robbery as a motive. "To think," Mrs. Munsinger wrote, "that all this time the neighborhood was harboring a degenerate."

Crystal read the newspaper clipping several times. The facts in isolation seemed strangely disembodied: simply a man found dead, his house ransacked, an investigation by the police. To read them meant nothing to her. But then the image came to her of Dr. Brightwood standing in front of his class, looking around in bewilderment as two students answered from different sides of the room. She could hear a buzz of comment and laughter as he told the tale of his fabulous exploration. It seemed to her at that moment that she had followed him down the corridor to his doom, she and all the others—had watched him all unknowing as he came to the edge and stepped over. And to her it had been given to follow his steps to the very last, to be involved without knowing it, watching helplessly while life happened to him. Horrified, she had to sit down. "Oh, poor man," she murmured. And she wondered if, before his wandering eye had been stilled forever, it had lit on anything that had even momentarily illuminated the chaos and allowed it to discover any sense in the world.

Reunion

"Well, Jarve, you old sinner, it's about time," Alison said as she met me on the porch. She gave me a little peck on the cheek, then stood back to make inspection. "You've gotten skinny as a rail, Jarve," she said, "and pretty thin on top. The years have begun to tell on you, Jarve."

"You haven't changed a bit, Al."

"Oh yes, I know," she said, with a crack of a smile. "Same nasty tongue I've always had. But come in. No reason for us to stand on the porch staring at each other like idiots. Alna will be here directly to tell you how ill-used she always is." Before she turned to go in, she gave me another quick going-over. "Little short of breath these days, are you?"

"I lost my cat."

"Oh," she said, and pretended not to understand. "You derive long-windedness from cat fur? Cats make me sneeze." She sneezed. "Even the idea of cats."

"He was nearly wild in the car," I explained.

"I can imagine," she said, having noticed the covered bird-cage next to my suitcase. "I can't say the bird would be too happy either. Must be continual warfare in the back seat—worse than the battle of the sexes."

"A mynah bird," I told her. "He talks. Name's Charlie. But anyway—" going back to the cat, "the moment I opened the door, he shot out. Wouldn't come when I called. Stopped and gave me a backward look over the shoulder and hotfooted it off as fast as he could go. I tried chasing him . . ."

"Just see he doesn't come in the house," she said. "I have

put in my last cleaning up animal doo-doo." Then she added, "Foolishness to chase anything."

She ought to know, I thought: five-foot-four and over two-hundred-fifty pounds. Already my malice was beginning to show. A bad sign. "Your personal philosophy?" I intended a dig.

"My personal philosophy," she said, underlining the words. "There is nothing in this world worth chasing—" She started in and held open the screen door while I gave thought to whether I should hunt for Tigger or wait for him to turn up on his own. I followed her in.

"Nothing in this world—" she went on, "neither love nor fame nor . . ."

"Truth?"

She snorted. "What's that anymore? No—'nor peace nor certitude nor light.' Spend your energy chasing around and all you get is a little pool of tears."

"Not getting cynical in your old age, are you, Al?" I said, upsetting a coat-tree as I bumped it with a suitcase.

"Me? What an idea."

"That's an heirloom," she reminded me, as I caught the coat-tree on its way down to the floor. "Been in the family for at least three generations."

"Well, I'd hate to break up the family tree," I said, whatever that meant, and stood blinking in the hallway, unable to see a thing.

"We keep the blinds drawn for coolness," she said, raising one at the front-room window. Motes of dust danced in the sunlight. I settled myself in a wingback chair, while she lowered herself into an overstuffed.

"Well, you recognize the old place?" she wanted to know. "Think you can claim it?"

Now that my eyes had adjusted to the light, the room began to take on a certain familiarity, though the furniture had been rearranged, a few things added, others gone. I crossed my legs, clasped my hands around my knee, and took a long look.

"That's Granddad's old school desk," she said. "They were going to get rid of it when they built the new school . . . Used to be a huge big old double desk, but Alna and I had it cut in half so we could each have one."

Leather-covered couch, wooden rockers, overstuffed chairs, the sort of things that would creak and scritch and groan when you sat in them, carrying on a conversation of their own, nearly all complaint. Drop-leaf table with the milk-glass plate and the shepherd and shepherdess exchanging coy looks across the polished surface. Family pictures on the wall, a crowd of silver and gold frames on the shelves, the desk, the mantel: including pictures of me. (But of course. The family never let go of you, never absolved you from being a member, but waited for the prodigal, who in some sense had never been allowed to leave.) Seth Thomas clock in the middle of the mantel, not running.

"Nothing's changed," I said. If anything new had been added, it had taken on the sentiment that stood behind the rest. The years she and Alna had kept the house, ever since Alna had become a widow, were a continuation of everything I could remember. The chairs had taken their shape; their feet had worn the design into the carpet, so that it was quite lost now. All the things there had been taken into the stream of their existence and become part of it. Nothing had really changed, but had just gone on, wearing down, wearing out. The room smelled of warmed sunlit dust. Suddenly sleepy, I had to fight down a yawn.

"It's smaller than I thought. I remember a much bigger house."

"It's big enough when you go to cleaning it. I've got so I don't want to clean up after anybody." She eased herself forward and heaved herself up out of the chair. "You can take a look around and freshen up while I get us a glass of something cold. I gave you your old room at the top of the landing."

Quite a bit smaller, I thought, and was almost afraid to look at my old room.

My room was under the eaves, corners cut out where the roof sloped down, the ceiling so low you always had the feeling you were going to bang your head. The house had settled badly, the door swinging wide of the frame, the floor like an inclined plane. I sat down on the white chenille spread, bedsprings squeaking, the mattress sagging into a hollow under me, and tried to see things clearly.

Some things happen under the sun; others are the gift of moonlight. And there are those that lie in the twilight that connects past and present—part dream, part memory. Here was the room I'd lived in: brass bed, bookcase, desk, bureau. But now they stood out too clearly, like furniture in a secondhand store, with all their scars and scratches. Dream and memory fled before the eyes of the large and obtuse stranger sitting in the boy's room. What connection had I to these objects that habit and sentiment, or the habit of sentiment, had preserved, not even really for me? Yet it was all there. Even a childish drawing tacked up on the wall. Where had they resurrected that from? I got up to look at it. It was a drawing of a man, but with wings where the arms ought to have been, as though I'd meant to draw an arm but the crayon had slipped and I'd drawn wings in order to make the best of a bad job. The drawing intrigued me.

A good way to get past your mistakes, I thought. Fly beyond them. Fix on wings like you'd meant to fly. Make things look like you'd meant them to be that way and no other. Who'd know the difference? I'd know, I thought. I'd know I'd been a damned fool and made a mess of things. Forget the wings if you don't know how to fly. I sat down on the bed again, staring down at the fragments of my life that lay around my feet. They stood in all the harsh glare that the room now did. Maybe some few things should be left unreclaimed in the twilight, seeing that you can't get rid of the others.

I thought of Winifred, the breakup of our marriage, the bitterness. It's quite a shock to witness that sudden explosion of passion after so many years of numbed feeling, like finding sudden life in a deadened nerve. You can be full of cynical blame—I was for a time. But what minute unspoken adjustments we must have made for each other over the years. My silence behind a newspaper or book; her absorption with the coffee hour after church, the sewing group, the bridge games. For each other we had the bills, the weather, the local gossip.

You come to the end of such things and finally you call them by their true name—failure. It's like living with fading eyesight or a loss of hearing—all happening so gradually you don't notice, till one day the world is in shadow and no birds sing. Then you know only what is lost, not how to get it back. You look at the woman who has put the peanut butter or the cheese spread on all those slices of bread, and opened up her legs at night—and you know failure.

I'd reached the point where I couldn't blame Winifred, though she took everything—the house, the furniture, the good car, the savings. I hadn't wanted any of it. Now that the life had flowed out of it, it was only rubbish, the flotsam of thirty years. The old wreck of a car, a few hundred dollars, the cat, and the bird were all I had left.

I avoided all my friends and acquaintances, didn't want to talk to anybody. I shed my old life like wrinkled skin, took the cat and the bird and moved into the Petite Apartments, one of the great old homes brutally subdivided in a neighborhood on the downslide from respectability. You made your way up to the porch past the garbage cans and the tricycles and toys lying in the middle of the sidewalk and all over the porch and entered into a decaying hallway. Just in time for a wife or kid getting slapped around or a hair-pulling fight between a couple of the women: shrieks and curses, cries and blows. After a while they became so much background noise, just as the smells of everybody's supper were simply the air you breathed. And even the faces . . . Who noticed? Except when the cops came looking for somebody who'd forged checks or skipped out on his bills. By that time, long gone. Faces changed, but nothing else. For a time, a little girl named Rachel knocked on my door every morning wanting milk, something to eat—her mother was always sick or asleep. Then they too were gone, and I was left to myself.

I had the idea that Tigger, Charlie, and I were going to create a new life together. I tried to get the cat and the bird to become friends and companions. I'd hold Tigger on my lap and pet him till he purred. Then I'd reach over and bring Charlie out of his cage, a little closer each time. I could tell Charlie was pretty nervous. But Tigger would just lie there and purr, with only a little twitch in the stick end of his tail.

One day I went out and left the two of them together, Charlie in his cage, which was hanging from the ceiling, and Tigger curled up in the chair. When I came back, Tigger was up there with Charlie, in midair with no place to go, clinging to the cage with all his claws. He'd leapt up from the table. I'd have been impressed by the leap if I hadn't been so quick to judge him. I gave him a cuff or two as I dropped him to the floor. He laid back his ears and whipped under the bed. After that he kept clear of me. Came in for his food, but that was it. The hunting was too deep in his blood for him to give it up, even for the sake of society. It was my fault. I'd been living in a dream. Trying to create the Peaceable Kingdom. But the cat wasn't ready to lie down with the mynah bird, and I'd have done better to get down on all fours myself.

About that time two things happened: an old woman, the only permanent renter of the Petite Apartments, died, and I figured out the nature of the smell in the hallway. The old woman was ninety-one, and she'd starved to death. Under her bed they found a can with $35,744.32 inside. The smell in the hallway that I'd gotten so used to was of many things rolled up in one: sweat and dirt and the damp behind the plaster, diapers soured in the pail and boiled cabbage and potatoes fried in lard. I hadn't been able to figure out what the smell was. But after the old woman died, suddenly I knew: it was the smell of failure and slow death. And when I knew that, I fled—back up here. Home.

"Jarve, come down and have some lemonade," Alison called. Then another voice. "Jarvis, guess who's here."

It was Alna. I left the suitcase half unpacked and went downstairs.

"Oh, Jarvis, Jarvis," Alna devoured me with her arms, smothering me in her bosom, and gave me a great wet sisterly kiss. "You've come back to us. You're a sight for sore eyes. Though I know you can't say the same of me. The years have been too hard on me, Jarve . . ."

I tried to protest. Actually, the years had left her a great soft rubbery mound, like her twin. Little red eyes that seemed on the verge of weeping, peering timidly from a great billow of fat. She seemed ageless; the skin of her face was as smooth as an infant's

"Don't say anything good about her," Alison put in, handing me a glass of lemonade. "She'll only have to work harder denying it."

"How long has it been, Jarve, since you've come to a reunion?" Alna asked as we sat down. "How wonderful you've come now—just in time. I used to think, he doesn't like us any more, doesn't want to have anything to do with us . . ."

"Now, Alna," I said, thinking, here we go again. "People drift apart. They get busy and . . ."

". . . stop caring any more," Alison said perfunctorily, reminding me of all the reasons I had stayed away.

"But now we have him back," Alna said—she'd had to draw a little blood. With a little guilt I could pay the price of reentry into her affection. "For the first time since before Corey's wedding. And you've never seen the babies—Annie and John and David or any of Dodie's kids, and . . ."

"I suppose Aggie will come," Alison said.

"Of course she will," Alna said, almost belligerently. "Why shouldn't she come?"

"Aggie has a new husband," Alison explained. "Smaller than the last. The only kind she marries are the ones she can pick up and throw."

"Well, it could have been worse," Alna said. "Just thank your lucky stars . . ."

"And worse it may be yet. The worst is not so long as we can say 'This is the worst.' " With a little smile she challenged us to match her book-learning.

"I see you can still bring out the Bard with the best of them," I said. "Well, I've been away a long time. I've lost track of my connections." All of them. Even Alna's three girls—

Corey, Dodie, and Aggie. Girls? Women now, still stuck with
the same ridiculous nicknames they'd been saddled with as
children. The youngest, Corey, had been like my own daughter. She was in fact the same age as our older girl. When they
were little she used to come down and stay with us for part of
the summer. Corey liked what she called "adventures," and
traveling a hundred miles or so on the bus by herself was an
adventure. A long time ago that had been. It was hard now to
bring everything up to date. Marriages, kids, divorces, second
marriages, what-all.

"Well, you went away," Alison said, as though pointing out
a moral fault. "The rest of us stayed behind mostly. They go,"
she said, perhaps to someone not present, but listening,
"though I don't know they're any better off for it. You look
like you've been picked clean down to the tail feathers, Jarve,"
she said, with her usual relish. "You look like you came here
on the run."

"You're a balm to the spirit, Al." Yes, indeed. Coming back
had its price. And how long did one go on paying?

"All I do is speak out what everybody else is afraid to say."

"Some people think they're being honest," Alna said,
"when all they're being is disagreeable."

Alison looked at her in surprise. "That's pretty good," she
said. "You're not going to get clever on us in your old age—"

"But the important thing," Alna said, sheering off, "is that
he's here—with us. And he'll stay, and it'll be just like it was
before she took him away from us—using her daddy's hardware store as a bait and a lure. Grandma never got over it."

"And what does that say about me?" I demanded.

"I'll bet she took you for plenty," Alison said.

"Come now," I said, "you've looked for reasons to dislike
Winifred ever since I first brought her home. Whatever she
took, I let her take."

"The more's the pity."

"She was never our sort," Alna said. "I knew things would
work out like this."

"But, Alna—" I tried to keep my temper. "—it was thirty
years. We had a whole life together."

"Pooh," she said, waving her hand, the fat of her upper arm quivering. "A woman knows those things. And I knew how anxious she was to marry our little brother. She didn't have the connections. And when the girls came along and she saw they'd be eligible . . ."

"Eligible?"

"For the DAR. For the FFV."

"What are you talking about? Where did you get such an idiotic notion?" It was awful—I hadn't been home an hour and already I was shouting.

"What have I done?" Alna wailed.

"I'm sorry. Please—just forget I said anything."

"You can hardly blame him," Alison said, turning on her as well. "Who cares about such rubbish? It's all down the drain anyway."

And with a sweep of her hand, she dismissed my past like a pan full of dirty water.

The next day was Memorial Day, the day the family reunion was always held, and half the county was on hand for the event. For everybody in those parts was connected to everybody else, and you were always discovering someone new who'd staked a claim on the remote borders of kinship. Seemed like hardly anybody ever left the area, but instead married and settled down to add another set of cousins to the total. And those few who picked up stakes to go back East or out West might as well have been numbered among the wayward, the lost, or the dead. All during the morning people kept swarming in and out of the house, the little kids chasing one another around a yard brilliant with roses and daylilies, while the teenagers stood off to one side, deep in themselves. Meanwhile, their folks drank coffee and visited, carrying on as though they hadn't seen one another for years, though half of them lived less than twenty miles away.

In years past, the picnic had been held in the park right on the bank of the Tippicanoe River, which makes a wide lazy bend right through the center. But now that Corey had her new house and lots of space they held the picnic there. I

hadn't seen Corey yet; I was anxious to know how she'd
turned out, she'd been such a favorite of mine.

"We'll go over early," Alna said, "so you can have a chance
to see the cemetery. Harley's done a lot with it."

"That so?" So far as I knew, there was only one thing you
could do with a cemetery.

I'd been wondering what sort of man Corey had ended up
with. I hadn't gone to her wedding. Guess I was afraid to.
Corey had wanted to go off to college in California, but Alna
wouldn't let her: she could go to college right here at home if
she wanted to. But Corey, who'd always had a stubborn
streak, said she wouldn't go at all if she couldn't go where she
wanted. Next thing I heard, she was getting married.

About noon Harley himself came over to fetch Alna. I was
to take Alison in my car. This was so that each could sit in the
front seat, since it would have baffled the ingenuity of any
driver to get either of them in or out of the back. Neither
could drive, and Harley's was a two-door model.

Harley was a short burly fellow with carrot-colored hair
and a round amiable face, rather mealy and freckled the way
of so many redheads. He shook hands with a grip that fell just
short of mashing together all the bones in my hand and gave
me a smile from a toothpaste ad.

"Been up since six," he announced. "Had to open a grave
and wanted to get it done before folks started coming and
bringing their flowers. Wouldn't have looked right." He was
one of the few left, he told me, who opened graves "by hand"
any more. And he showed me his arm, which was as thick and
solid as the average man's leg. "Feel that," he said. "Hard as a
rock. It's what comes of digging graves. I can dig one in an
hour. If you tried it, or most folks, you'd be in one."

"Harley, you're bragging," Alison said.

He grinned and rocked back on his heels.

"Don't know what we'd do without Harley," Alna said. "He
does all the yard work, and whatever breaks down he puts
back together. He can fix anything."

"By the way, Harley," Alison said, "we're having trouble
with the sink letting out. Gone sluggish again. It's probably
tree roots in the sewer."

"I'll check it over right now. I've got my tools in the car—always keep 'em handy." And he dashed off to get them.

"Obliging fellow, I will say that for him," Alison said.

Alna took this as a cue for praise: Harley was not a man to sit idle. He was strong as an ox and cheerful as a sunbeam. He built houses and dug graves and carved monuments and worked part-time for an electrician. Never idle.

"Not one of your types to sit behind a desk exercising a pencil," Alison said, in time for Alna to add: "You can say that again."

"Yes," Alison said, "Harley is a man who knows what he wants and knows how to get it."

Which was more than I did.

He stood there entirely at home with himself, Alna beaming over him, her son-in-law, and Alison willing to make use of him.

"I'll ream her out this afternoon while you all are playing canasta."

"You've got a lot of energy," I said—which was true.

"Everything he touches turns to money," Alna said, admiringly.

"He's got the first nickel he ever made," Alison said to me as we were going out. "He'll be a rich man any minute."

As we drove down Grant Street with its great old houses, Alison reminded me of the families that had lived in them nearly half a century ago. She could recall all the names of those who, for me, had slipped out of sight and memory, the kids we'd played with and gone to school with; knew what had happened to them since and who they'd married and where they'd gone. Since I left, the town had spread out in all directions, frantically adding new developments as though it couldn't wait to become a city. I hardly recognized the old center of town.

The families were gone from the old houses, where signs indicated the nests of lawyers, doctors, real-estate brokers, and insurance agents who had taken over, installed wall-to-wall carpeting, and set up for business.

We left the houses behind and traveled along a dirt road for perhaps half a mile.

"You remember the old part of the cemetery," Alison said, "where all the Butterworths and Waggoners are buried— Great-uncle Jed and Frank as well as Granddad. Mom and Dad are at this end just on the other side of the road."

"Which part is Harley's?"

"That's on past. Can't see it for the hill. He bought the land to make a private cemetery. Only the town was running out of room and wanted to buy it from him. He was too smart to sell. So now the town leases the land from him and he's gravedigger, caretaker, the whole works. Here, turn up this drive."

We drove up to a large ranch-style home, set right on top of the hill, commanding a view of the green swath below, where artificial wreaths made gaudy spots of color on the grass. Corey's house. Harley had built it himself. Not only did it have all the modern conveniences, but, as Alison observed, it had the advantage of being close to his work. I helped Alison from the car, and we walked to the door accompanied by the chimes of "Rock of Ages," being piped out by an amplifier on the corner of the house.

"Oh, Uncle Jarve," Corey cried when she saw me, throwing her arms around my neck. "Oh, it's so wonderful to see you. Come in."

She gave Alison a quick kiss. "I tell you, those kids are about to wear me out. This is John," she said, giving the little boy a twitch on the shoulder. He was about five—carrot-colored hair like his dad's. "Now you take your truck outside and behave yourself and tell David to behave. Where's Mother anyway?" she demanded of Alison. "Why isn't she around when you need her? Make yourselves at home," she said in a hurried way. "I've got to see about the potato salad. Go on now," she said to John, "and you stay right where I can keep my eye on you."

"She's on tranquilizers," Alison said in a low voice, "though what earthly good they're doing I can't imagine. Come," she said. "We can take a little walk before things get started. Bundle of nerves," she murmured.

When we got outside, Harley and Alna had come up. "You'd better go in and lend some aid and comfort to your daughter," Alison said.

I let Alison lead me off, so that I wouldn't allow myself to dwell on the disappointment I felt deep within. Corey, this harried woman? Was there anything left of the Corey I remembered?

Alison knew the cemetery the way she knew the town. A living archive. And she ticked off the graves one after another. "That's Great-uncle Jed buried there. He lived the longest—a hundred and five. The Ridpaths are nearly all of them over here. Three of Granddad's brothers. The oldest went West and was never heard from again."

"You mean somebody left?"

"There's always a restless one in the lot. And there's Granddad."

"Josiah Ridpath," I read. A good strong name, I thought, trying to make out the dates where the weather had discolored the stone. Name for a patriarch, the builder of a line. For his time he'd been outstanding. A farmer, but an educated man: superintendent of schools when the Democrats were in power; teacher when they weren't. The family still voted Democrat—it was a tradition. And he'd sent both my father and my uncle to college. "Maybe they knew what they were doing when he was alive."

"You think so?" Alison said. "When have they ever? And I remember what he was like. You were too young. He took up all the room, and the rest of the world was background and decoration. Oh, he was civic-minded, all right. But when did Grandma ever have a thought of her own?"

"He lived by his lights," I said. "You have to say that for him."

"Yes, a man of principle. Stubborn and high-minded. When in doubt, do right. Well, I suppose you save a lot of confusion and wasted energy."

A rock, that's what he was. To be relied on. Even his memorial had something hard and substantial about it, monumental. Maybe that's why I came back. What would he have thought looking at me? ("Degenerate sons and daughters, life is too strong for you.") The same thing he must have thought about my dad, very likely. Who had gone off to college bearing the hopes of the family, but who, instead of becoming the minister they reckoned on, threw his life away as a musician. Even went off to New York for a time. But he came back finally, unable to earn a living, and became organist for the local Methodist church, giving lessons on the side and playing the violin for occasional evening gatherings. Died not long after I was born. And now here I was. Aloud I said, "Once I had the right way. Now I don't seem to have any way. Guess you're the clear-sighted one in this generation. You haven't botched things up the way some of us have."

"No, I s'pose not. I just get to watch the rest of the world go at it—that is my exalted privilege."

By the time we got back to the house, little clusters of people were all over the yard, with fresh arrivals coming up the hill every minute. Picnic tables had been set up alongside the garage, paper plates and napkins weighted down with pickle jars and catsup bottles to keep the breeze from sweeping them down the hill. The tables were loaded with food: chicken and noodle casseroles with crust on the top and gravy oozing through, and piles of ham and fried chicken and pots of baked beans and marshmallow jello salads and macaroni salads and coleslaw and cream pies and cherry pies and angel cakes and pans of brownies and a great lovely strawberry shortcake with whipped cream on the top. A real winner. I staked that one out right away, wondering how I could grab a piece before everybody else beat me to it. And right as I had my eye on it, Corey's boy John reached up and took a fistful out of the top, as much cake and strawberry as he could grab.

"John! You little beast! What have you done?"

John, struck with mortal terror by the voice that had come suddenly out of nowhere, did not even put the fistful of strawberries into his mouth. He just stood there while Corey dashed out of the kitchen and whacked him hard on the side of the head. He stumbled as she yanked him into the house bawling, a smear of whipped cream across his cheek.

Some few looked up momentarily from their conversations. None of their affair. But something contracted inside me, and suddenly all the fried chicken and ham and salad and beans and pies and cakes that you could dive into and come out on the other side of, feeling cheerful and at one with all those folks, was just food. Still, I heaped up a plate with everything it would hold and ate it down like food was going out of fashion; and then it all sat like lead on my stomach, pulling me to the downhill side of the afternoon.

I was weary. I'd just about worn out my jaw. No sooner did I lift the fork to my mouth than somebody'd ask me a question and I'd have to fill him in about my history. And there, fresh in memory, were all the things I'd have been glad to forget. But that wasn't the worst. I had to listen to all the codgers who knew everything that had ever happened in the family and who could not forget or leave out a single scrap. "Your daddy was tall and skinny like you. Sickly. And when you were growing up . . ." History was everywhere. I was in the middle of it, no escaping. All down the hill it lay. And I felt giddy, like I was being absorbed backward into it, devoured by ghosts.

I sought comfort in the present generation. I found my other niece, Dodie, with her kids in tow, who looked a comfortable matron, rather heavy, working on a double chin. I learned the names of the kids and the grades they were in, I heard about their new house and her husband's job, and then we took refuge in the weather.

"Where's Aggie?" I asked. "I haven't seen her yet."

"You can never tell about Aggie. She may turn up or she may not." She shrugged, as though whatever Aggie did, it was all the same to her.

"And I don't see Corey. I'll bet she hasn't even eaten yet." That gave me a chance to escape. If I went inside the house, at least I wouldn't have to talk to anybody for a while. Or else I could talk to Corey, if that's where she was. I hadn't seen her since she dragged the little fellow off. I found her sitting on the lounge in the living room with the child beside her, asleep. His face was flushed from crying, and every now and then his breath would catch in a sob and send a tremor through his sleep. I could see that Corey had been weeping.

"What's the matter, honey?"

"I don't know why I hit him like that," she said, the tears streaming down her cheeks. "I must be crazy." She dabbed at her eyes with a wadded Kleenex. "What did it matter if he took a hunk out of the cake? Seems like every time they do anything, all I know is to beat on them."

I sat down beside her and took her hand. "It's hard raising kids. You never know whether to blame yourself for the things you've done or the things you didn't do." Then I thought, that's a helluva lot of comfort.

"Oh, why am I so terrible?" she said. "I feel so restless. I fly off the handle at nothing—I feel like I want to hit somebody or break something."

I held her hand. What was I supposed to tell her? To get some hobbies or improve her bridge game? What had happened to her? She'd been such a great kid—wonderful. Where had it all leaked away? And why? I had to ask it, even though I was hardly in any position to think: she's a disappointment to me.

"Something's wrong with me," she said. "It just seems like I'm missing—oh, I don't even know what. Oh, Uncle Jarve, it's terrible not knowing—driving me crazy. Maybe if I'd gone away and been to college like I wanted, I'd know. Oh," she cried, leaning on my shoulder, "I'm an old woman, and I'm not even thirty."

She dabbed at her eyes again and blew her nose. "I'm glad you're here," she said. "You're the only person . . ." Then she turned to me with an expression I recognized from her childhood: serious, full of question, as though she'd been turning something over in her mind for a long time. "You went to college, you went away . . ." she began.

"But all I ever did was run a hardware store," I said, "in another little town. As for my education—it kept me away from the *Reader's Digest Condensed Books* and allowed me to concoct my own set of private miseries as a reaction to what's wrong with the world."

"But why did you come back?"

"I don't know, honey," I said, genuinely puzzled. "I guess I was scared, maybe scared enough to forget the reasons I'd left in the first place."

"Are you going to stay, Jarve?" she said, looking at me intently. When she said it, dropping the *uncle* and looking at me like that, some part of myself seemed to be sitting in front of me putting me to the test.

"I don't know, honey."

I had to get up at that point and move around. Why had I left? Why had I come back? What was I going to do? "I guess there's always been something in me that could never get along in the world," I said, thinking out loud. "Especially when I was a kid. There was always something else, at the back of my eyes that I could see, even it if wasn't really there—like a dream. I thought it was gone. But it's always been there, under all the patchwork and fabrication I've put on top of it for the past quarter of a century—God, longer than that."

"A dream," she said excitedly, "and you still have it?"

"I guess." If that's what you could call my dissatisfaction— the restlessness, the itch in the blood. If you could glorify it with the name *dream*. I thought I'd outgrown whatever it was: thought the surface of my life had got too thick a deposit on it for anything to break through. Even now that all was cracked and broken and the darkness had welled up, was there reason to hope for light?

"Then you won't stay," she said. "Oh, I knew it."

"Hold on, wait a minute." She was about to snatch the rug out from under me. "Where can I go, for God's sake?"

"Oh, thank you, Jarve."

"Thank you for what?" The taste of acid was on my tongue.

"You give me hope. You make me believe I don't have to be a failure."

I could have wept. "All you're thanking me for is misery— for troubles you can't even give a name to."

"Oh, you make me want to hug you." No doubt she would have if the child hadn't been on her lap.

From outside, somebody said, "Where's Corey? Haven't seen her all afternoon."

"They'll come in," she said, gathering up the child, who'd sat up and was rubbing his eyes. "Come on in to the bathroom, honey. Tell them I'll be out in a bit," she said, and carried him quietly down the hall.

"Where's Corey?" Alna said, coming in, Harley at her heels.

"She's missing all the fun. When everybody clears out, we'll have a little canasta."

"I'm going on over to see about the sewer," Harley said, "soon as I get out of these clothes."

"You'll miss all the fun," I said.

"My work's my pleasure," he said with satisfaction, and left me only the comfort of a nice bit of irony.

"You'll have to explain things to me," I said. "I haven't played this game for years." And didn't want to now. With a little less sleep and a rawer state of nerves, I might have made it as far as hatred and violence. As it was, I settled for a sort of low-grade irritability. Corey and I both had been roped into playing. We made suitable partners.

" Pooh, it's simple," Alison said. "Even we can play it."

"Al's used to winning," Corey said.

"Well now, don't discourage him at the outset," Alison said. "I haven't got luck trapped in a corner."

"I've never seen anybody like her," Corey said. "The cards go her way."

The discard pile was beginning to mount as we kept going round the table. And the tension was building. Even I got into the game. The cards kept mounting up—nobody had enough to meld—to the point where the pile was worth taking. So I took it. Alison discarded a five; I had two of them and the points to open.

"Now just look at that," Alna said.

"Yes, just look at that," Alison said. "I had my eye on that stack. Been sitting here with the points just waiting for the right card." And she reached over and pinched me.

A right sharp pinch, as though she'd meant it to hurt, and she sat there looking ruffled and displeased. Why, she really does want to win, I thought, spreading out another run. And my blood was up—I wanted to beat her just for the sake of triumph. Now there was real zest in the play that seemed to raise both sight and hearing almost to animal keenness. I became aware of Alison's breathing, even thought I could hear her heart pumping. And there was Corey taking the next fat pile, which included Alna's joker, a sacrifice.

"Now look at that, will you," Alison said, giving me another pinch. "Why, they mean to take everything."

"Not leaving anything for us," Alna moaned.

And I thought, if I take that pile again, the buttons will pop off the front of her dress. It was worth trying for. Ah, the joy of battle!

"I got it this time," Alna said, swooping up the pile gleefully. But it was thin pickings.

"At least we'll have a book of tens. They won't romp all over us."

"And I'm going to make two more black canastas," Alison said, "before they go out."

When the hand ended, we were far ahead, and the next two went with a rush of luck for Corey and me. I glanced over to see what the score was, but we were ahead by a surprisingly small margin—only about fifteen hundred points. Had she added wrong? No, Alison never added wrong. We were winning, but now I had to beat them mercilessly. We had to take the pile every chance we got.

"Oh, Uncle Jarve," Corey said. "You're doing wonderfully. I bet we're over three thousand points ahead."

That didn't help matters.

"Just you wait," Alison said. "Just you wait." She was drumming her fingers on the table, so I thought I was reasonably safe. Then I nearly leapt from the table, she pinched me so hard. Alna got me from the other side.

The pile was building up again, and Alna and Alison, sitting across from each other, were two great cats watching it with narrow eyes, waiting. . . .

"Hello, everybody, here I am. Where's all the food?" Opening the door, sweeping into the room like a hot wind, there was Aggie. She was carrying a sackful of lettuce, which she set down on the floor. "Well, Uncle Jarve. Fancy meeting you here. They've roped you into a card game already." She plopped herself into a chair and sat rocking back and forth, her knees spread apart. She gave the impression that she was enjoying herself hugely.

"Why, Aggie," Alna said, "what are you doing here this time of day?"

I had seen Alna flinch when she came in, a protest of flesh, an unconscious squirm with a long history. For Aggie had been a wild child and not a credit to the family. It was rather a miracle she'd graduated from high school, before flunking out or being kicked out. Whooping it up half the night on the back roads with the boys, coming to school the next day and sleeping on her desk. Flinging into class in a skimpy blouse, barefooted, bells around her ankles, and being sent home with stern warnings. Yelling across the study hall to the drama teacher, her favorite, "Oh, Ella, Aunt Ella, I'm pregnant. What'll I do?" Running off with a folk singer right after graduation; returning home three years later with a child and no husband. A second marriage, a third, a fourth. And still untamed. All that lay behind Alna's squirm.

"You're only half a day late," Alison said. "Didn't think you'd be coming."

"Neither did we. Elton'll be here in a minute. I brought eggs—hen eggs and goose eggs. You should see my gray geese. Proud and fat. Strut all over the yard." She got up, put her arms akimbo and strutted around the room. "My gray geese are like my children."

"And your children?" Alison said, dryly. "What are they like?"

"Well, Auntie," she said, not the least abashed. "I haven't even seen them for three years now. The abandoned little orphans. They're well taken care of. Henry can feed 'em and clothe 'em same as I."

"I wish I could take things as lightly as you. Run off devil-may-care."

"It's a gift, Auntie," she said, and laughed. "Now I have my gray geese and my teddy bear."

Her teddy bear was a thin little runt of a man, whose hair shot off into a cowlick at the back of his head. He held out a limp damp paw for me to shake, pumped my hand a time or two, gave a little nod and a friendly grunt, then sat back on the couch, having done his bit for sociability. Aggie dwarfed him, both in size and voice; she boomed—she filled a room. Whatever her other husbands had been, this time she'd pawed around in the back patches of Mother Nature till she'd found one witless and pliable enough to do her bidding.

"Now bring in the eggs, Elton," she said, "and mind you don't drop 'em."

"How are things with you, Aggie?" Corey asked.

"Can't complain. Put in tobacco again this year. The allotment's small, but it'll be worth money. Got a little corn and a little alfalfa. Got a pig and three goats and half a dozen sheep and a cow and my gray geese. I work from first light till nearly dark. See my hands," she said, holding them out. "Rough—from digging in the dirt."

"Honest work," Alison said, though which way her irony cut was hard to tell.

"Yes, Auntie. I was always the one for clean living." She broke into a great peal of laughter.

Elton came in with the eggs and took them into the kitchen. We'd stopped playing when Aggie came in, but there was no move to break up the game. "Discard," Alna said. "You're holding up the game," Alison said. So I played.

"There's food in the kitchen," Corey said. "Plenty left in the refrigerator. Just help yourselves."

They both brought in plates of food and ate it and talked while we played cards. Then, quite as abruptly as she'd come in, Aggie stood up to leave. "Well, we got to be going," she announced. "Going to have us a little night out. No, don't anybody get up, we can find our way to the door." Actually, nobody'd made a move in that direction. "Come, love," she beckoned. "'Bye all. Just wanted to pay our respects to the family. Have fun, Uncle." She gave me a wink and swept out of the room, Elton in tow, carried along, it seemed, by the power of her voice alone.

"Well, looks like she's getting along all right with her new husband," Alna said, determined to stay on the sunny side of life.

"I should hope so," Alison said. "Why, she'd squash him flat if he looked at her the wrong way."

Alna's face flushed.

"Aggie never had any moral sense," Alison went on, freezing the pile.

"She never had any sense, period," Corey said.

"I raised my girls to be good girls," Alna protested, close to tears.

"Well, Aggie ducked out on you—ducked out on the teacher and the preacher both."

All that energy, I thought. Given the right direction she ought to have been able to fly to the moon.

"She's a disgrace," Corey said.

"That may be," Alison said. "But she's also your sister."

"Yes, I have to remember that, don't I? Because you'll put me down if I forget."

"Don't be impertinent, miss," Alison said, as though Corey were nine years old.

"She *is* a disgrace," Corey insisted. "Not to the family or to me—you think I care about that? She's a disgrace to herself."

The frustration and pent-up feeling catalyzed by Aggie's appearance filled the room, and Alna and Alison were staring at her as though she'd gone crazy: she was making a spectacle of herself.

"And what might you know about that?" Alison said, tactlessly.

"And what right do you have—?" Corey yelled, roused to fury. "You can't even add."

"What?"

"You added the score all wrong. We have another seven hundred points you didn't give us, plus all the rest."

"Corey!" Alna said. "How dare you?"

"It's true. I've always known. And I've been watching." Turning to Alison. "I know how you win."

Despite her efforts to remain composed, Alison was visibly shaken. "Coretta Jean, I'm going to leave this house and I'll not come back until—"

"Until what?" Corey said, pushing back the chair, standing up. "Until I get down on my knees and beg?"

"Well, I got the roots out," Harley announced triumphantly, man against nature. He'd come in so quietly through the back door we hadn't heard him. There he was, smiling, grease and dirt on his clothes and hands, a smudge of grease across his forehead.

Corey looked at him, made a gesture as though it was all hopeless.

"Well, I guess I don't look like an ice-cream salesman," he said.

"Oh, go clean up."

"What's the matter, honey?" he said, bewildered. "What'd you expect a man to look like who's been cleaning out a sewer?"

"Will you clean up, you big slob," she said, sweeping the cards off the table. "Mother, I'll drive you home. I want to talk to you."

Harley's face paled, leaving his freckles without any visible means of support.

Alna was weeping. "How could you do that? How could you?"

"Goddamn it to hell," Corey yelled.

"What's wrong?" Harley wanted to know. "What's happened?"

"Oh, God," Corey whispered. "Oh, God."

The house originally owned by my grandparents and now inhabited by the twins had never been what you would call fancy. Not one of those fine old houses with gingerbread along the porch and stained-glass windows along the stairwell or leaded glass in the front door. New, it had been ordinary; now it was old, with a patchwork of things done to it to keep it standing—asbestos shingles laid over the weathered exterior, aluminum storm windows installed with the hope of reducing the drafts, a new electric stove in the kitchen, but the same old plumbing, endlessly repaired. From time to time a new layer of wallpaper over the old, a new coat of paint on the woodwork. Ordinary, comfortable, threadbare, but hanging on. Only now when we got back, there was an air of desolation about it, what with each person cut off from the rest by feelings too powerful for himself, let alone anybody else.

Alison and I got back long before Corey brought Alna home. I lay down for a while, heavy and depressed, and dozed off. When I woke it was fully dark outside. I sat up, shook my head free of sleep, then got up without turning on the light. For a time I stood looking out the window, trying to put something together. Family. Granddad. The twins. I couldn't put anything straight, couldn't line them up like portraits along a wall. Corey's outburst reverberated in my head. Loss. Waste. Betrayal. My father. And I. Who, what were the failures? And which was worse—the betrayal of others or of oneself?

I became aware of a confused babble of voices rising from below, wail and argument: Corey and Alna. "I want to be something," I heard from one of the outbursts, "before I'm buried."

In the quiet that followed, I heard Alison say, "A celebrity? A femme fatale?"

I heard the door slam, and the house settled into silence. I turned on the light, sat down on the edge of the bed. I don't know how long I sat there not thinking of anything, until I realized that I'd been staring at the winged man. A curious creature with its triangular wings and a face too innocent even for hope. Had the boy merely been attempting to leap past a wrong move? Or had he been yearning toward some as-yet unguessed possibility? And had the man unknowingly brushed past it, let it slip away all unheeded? Forever gone. Or might one still . . . ? I hardly dared ask the question—and yet not to ask it . . . Oh God, I thought. The waste. The terrible waste.

But what was the good of sitting there? If I was going to botch things up, hell, I might as well do a job of it. Perhaps Corey at least . . . And if she believed in what I could scarcely believe in myself . . . .

I went to the closet and pulled out my suitcase. Now was as good a time as any. When I went downstairs to the living room, Alna and Alison were sitting opposite one another in the overstuffed chairs. Alna was weeping.

"All my children have treated me this way—like dirt. And their father, out of his mind half the time."

"Well, you married him," Alison reminded her, "against the wishes of the family. And went on living with him—"

"Oh, how can you—when I'm in all this trouble? Her just leaving him flat out. A good marriage, the children, that beautiful home."

"Well," Alison said, "they're all doing it these days. Life goes on, eh, Jarve?"

"Well, you're the philosophical one," I said, on my way to the door. Alison looked at the suitcase but didn't comment.

"With a house like that, you'd think she could put up with anything," Alna wailed.

"Maybe she should have gone to California like she wanted," Alison said, her voice following me out the door, "and got all the nonsense worked out of her system."

"You're the one who always knows the right thing to do," Alna cried, "—for everybody else. And what have you ever done?"

I put the suitcase in the car and walked back upstairs to get the cage with Charlie. He hopped around nervously when I lifted up a corner of the cover. He wasn't used to being moved around at night.

"Where are you going, Jarve?" Alna said, looking up with red eyes.

"I don't know, my dear," I said, leaving a small kiss on top of her head. "If the cat turns up, take care of him for me. Corey'll be all right," I said. Fat lot of comfort. I gave Alison a little wave as I departed. "Maybe you'll be back," she said wryly.

I had noticed that Corey's car was still parked in front of my old wreck, but I didn't know where she'd gone. She came walking up as I put the bird in the back seat.

"Well," she said, with a little smile and a shrug.

"Well," I said, in the same spirit.

"Oh, Jarve, I hope you understand me."

"Of course," I assured her. "It's hard when you can't offer a solid proposition, a bet with reasonable odds if not a sure thing—when all you've got is a guess and a prayer."

"It isn't that I want to run off and screw a bunch of guys or get a job with an advertising agency. It isn't that at all. But . . . Oh, I don't know. I'm just groping in the dark."

"I know," I said. She had company.

"I'm glad you're leaving," she said.

"Well, good luck, darling," I said, putting my arms around her.

Unable to speak, she kissed me and left without another word.

Outside, the night was brilliant with stars. I took a deep breath that lifted heart and lungs. The air smelled of moisture, of things growing in the soil, reaching for their summer. Too bad, I thought, that one had lost so much of the animal he could no longer catch the scent of something fresh in the wind. The smell of earth was reassuring, yet maddening and depressing. What would draw me bounding into that promise? My wings were wet and sticky; I was still weak and unready.

I thought of those who were staying behind, visited by rain and snow and all the varying weathers of experience. I could have stayed with them, under the illusion of safety; but it was too late for that. At least I knew where I had gotten my restlessness. I'd held it down for thirty years—now I was a leaf in the wind.

The Ink Feather

From inside, their voices rose, interlocked in quarrel. Adrian shouting as he always did, Mama protesting in her ragged way. She's fighting back, Willa told her dolls, Clarise and Isabelle, without conviction, as she sat on the swing in the little enclosed porch, where she had been taking out their appendixes. She had cut their sides open, taken out something that looked like a chicken heart, and sewed them up again. The hard-edged words of her brother's anger made her think of stones a mean boy once had thrown at her, and she could see her mother holding up her hands as though to fend them off, trying to make her voice into a wall. But it wasn't strong enough—there were breaks. The words were arrows that hit and stuck. And sometimes the voice began to fall away and die, barely able to make it into words—watery syllables. Then Mama would gather her forces, and the two of them would be at it again.

Clarise and Isabelle sat with painted smiles as though their operation had put them beyond the cares of the world. And Willa forgot them. Her ears had grown in the direction of the quarrel.

"Can't you at least try to be a human being? Surely you can find something better to do than watch soap operas and eat junk. The house is a mess."

"You weren't supposed to come home till Thursday," Mama protested. "You don't know what it's like to suffer—the agony in my back, and my hip."

"The same old excuses."

Adrian was scolding Mama as he always did for being so

lazy and slow-moving and not keeping up the house. For every time she picked something up, she just turned around and set it down somewhere else, and nothing ever got put away. It meant nothing was ever lost, Mama said, though it seemed nothing was ever found, either. "It's here somewhere," she would say, rummaging through this pile and that until something else distracted her. Meanwhile, Adrian stood by, looking as though he wanted to tear the place apart and shake her till the stuffing came out. Willa could see it flying off in all directions.

Willa thought of how huge and soft Mama was, like a great pillow. "It's my thyroid," Mama always said, adding that when she was young she could touch the fingertips of her two hands around her waist. Now she was fifty-seven, terribly old, and Willa had been born late in her life. She wouldn't believe she was pregnant till it was almost time for the baby to arrive. "It was just as much a shock to me as it was to everybody else," Mama was fond of saying. "It wasn't supposed to happen, right in the middle of the change. I hadn't had a period for nearly half a year. I thought it was a tumor."

"What's a tumor?" Willa wanted to know.

"A growth, honey, and if you don't take it out, it kills you."

But she'd been in there all the time, growing inside her mother's stomach, but not so anybody could tell—a secret, just growing. If she'd been a tumor, she wouldn't have come out and been herself at all. And how strange that would have been, not to be in the world, but maybe even stranger to have been a tumor and grown till Mama died. She was glad she had made the right choice.

Only she wasn't sure. Maybe she hadn't done the right thing to come into the world. Even Mama seemed to be of two minds: sometimes she was pleased about it and sometimes she wasn't. When she was pleased, she'd say:

"Just think of having a baby at that age—when I ought to be a grandmother. There's life in the old girl yet." And she'd laugh.

But Adrian was never amused. "You're obscene," he would say. "How dare you? You came from the same place. But then you don't understand anything. You'll be all right when you get married, if you ever do. Maybe if you had a little fun yourself, you wouldn't be such a killjoy. Ah, if Frank had only lived . . ."

"All I need is a woman," Adrian had said sarcastically. "As though things aren't bad enough with the two of you around. At least Adam and Eve did something original," he said, pleased with his own wit. "God knows she made everybody suffer for it."

"And you're above it all. Think you're too good to be human. And what would you be, pray tell? Just because you've been to college . . . And what has it done for you except give you a better vocabulary for your nastiness?"

"Maybe if you kept your eye on something besides that idiot box you'd learn a thing or two," Adrian said over and over. And now he was saying what he always said: "But then you never did have a grain of sense."

Willa wanted to get up and go away, outside and down the alley to see Mary Anne. But it was winter outside, and gray clouds hung over the whole world. And she was forbidden to go down the alley: she might stray off and get lost. The devil lived below the ground down in the alley, and if he saw you, he would come up and beat you with his stick. That was what Mama told her once when she'd wandered off. And once a man had been found in the alley beaten up so badly there was barely life in his body. He didn't know what had happened to him. But Willa knew that the devil had done it. Even so, she liked to walk down the alley along the backyards of people's houses, though she was afraid the devil might get her.

Once back when she could barely remember, she had wandered off into an old stable. It smelled of hay and horses, a strong sweet smell of earth, though it was empty and the boards were broken in. And there she'd seen the black-and-white striped animal. She'd followed it out through the broken door saying "Kitty, here, kitty." But it had walked slowly away from her and disappeared.

She'd been punished when she came home: no one knew where she'd gone.

"You were just lucky," Adrian said, when she told about the animal. "If you'd been hit by that skunk, you'd have had to sleep outside for the rest of your life."

And they marveled that the skunk had not sprayed her.

For a long time after that, she was good and didn't wander off and tried to be neat and tidy and to be a help to Mama, who couldn't move fast and was always complaining about her back and legs. But no matter what she did, she had the secret knowing that the eye that looked upon her turned away in disgust. For it inevitably found her picking her nose or biting her nails or wiping her mouth on her sleeve or dropping bits of food onto the carpet. One night, Mama turned red and scolded her till the tears came for what she was doing under the covers.

Then one day it happened without her even thinking. It was summer, and she was in the yard with nothing to do. She started to chase a swallowtail that flitted just beyond her in a dance of pause and flight each time she tried to sneak up on it. When she looked around again, she couldn't see her house. Then she saw a little girl watching her. She had blonde hair that caught the light when it moved and pale blue eyes, and she was thin and could run fast. Her name was Mary Anne, and she lived near where the houses ended and the fields opened up and the trees stood against the sky.

That day they had rescued the rabbit. They had seen it, both in the same instant, being carried off by a black tomcat with a white nose and a torn ear and two yellow eyes that burned his seeing into whatever he looked at. He was advancing down the alley when they saw him with the bit of fur in his jaws. He gave them a quick look, about to dodge away with his prize. In that instant Willa saw that it was a rabbit, just a baby, and before she thought she made a rush at the cat. And the little girl, too, came running out of her yard. The cat ran under a bush, and they trapped him there against a wall. They tried to make him let go, while he clawed at them and growled and tried to sink his teeth deeper into the little rabbit. At last the cat leapt away with a yowl and left them with his victim.

The little girl held the creature in her hand, stroking its

fur, while Willa threw a handful of pebbles after the cat to scare it off.

"You're safe now, little rabbit," she crooned. "We saved you." But it lay still in her hand.

"Is it dead?" Willa asked, anxiously, breathlessly. It would be terrible if it were dead.

"No," said the little girl. "I can feel its heart. Maybe it's just frightened." She set it down on the ground and stepped back. Willa held her breath, watching. For a long moment the rabbit didn't move. Then suddenly it was leaping away.

"Be more careful next time, little thing," the girl said. And then to Willa: "Come and play. I'll tell you a dream I had."

How Willa escaped a whipping when she got home was a miracle to her. But Mama hadn't missed her, and Adrian was deep in his study with the door closed. She had come home with such dread that her fear sat like a great stone on her chest. She had not been found out, but what would happen if she got away with it? She was pulled between wanting to tell and get it over with and dreading what Adrian would say or do if she confessed. She stood for a long time in front of the door to his study wanting to knock. Once she got her hand almost to the door.

She even felt the stirring of an old curiosity. Only once had she ever been inside. Adrian never allowed anyone to enter his study, not even Mama, for she might break something valuable when she dusted, or else mess up his papers. But Willa could look inside if she was careful not to make any noise. Otherwise, he would roar, "Can't you see that I'm working? Go out and play, will you?"

The walls were covered with shelves of books that looked very old, with gold letters on the backs. And they had an old smell about them. Adrian managed a shop in which he sold them and other things as well—all old things. For some people wanted them more than they wanted new things and paid a lot of money for them. Sometimes he traveled to foreign lands and came back with things so rare and precious that hardly anyone could afford to buy them. Once in a while, he would come home in great spirits, saying that a certain collector had bought the such-and-such. "He has millions, of course. A mere trifle for him." When Willa tried to imagine such a human being, she thought of money stacked up to the ceiling.

There were figures on the shelves, carved of ivory and ebony wood, Adrian had told her. He had a great desk of dark wood where he sat and wrote letters and did arithmetic with big numbers. Under his chair was a white sheepskin rug. A large green blotter lay across the desk where Adrian wrote, always with an old-fashioned ink pen, in lines straight across the page or in long columns down it. She had watched him that one time and thought how neat and beautiful his writing was. She wished she could write like that instead of in the big stumpy, crooked letters that came out of her pencil and slanted down the page.

She had come home from school with her report card that one time, and he had called her in so he could look at it. She had gotten C's in arithmetic and reading, so that he was neither pleased nor displeased. And after he looked at the card, he didn't tell her right then to go out and play. She remained standing on the rug, white and fleecy beneath her feet, and watched him dip his pen into the crystal inkwell with the little brass top and write as though he were writing directions for the world. She looked around at the shelves with their carved figures that could have been people or animals, she wasn't sure. Quite without thinking, she pointed to one and said "What's that?" And Adrian took down an ivory figure, a dancing lady with flowers at her feet. She mustn't touch, and she held her breath before the delicate object lest she break it simply by breathing on it. It looked very old. Then she went out before Adrian told her to go. And her heart gave a little leap because he hadn't mentioned anything she had done wrong.

Now it was as though Mama were the child who had done wrong and must be scolded. Mama was crying. Willa could hear Adrian's voice descending like a club.

"Your own mother," Mama wept. "How can you treat me like this?"

"It's just what you deserve. If you weren't so stupid . . ."

Willa wanted to take Mama in her arms and rock her and sing to her as she sang to her dolls. She went to the door and opened it.

"What do you want?" Adrian demanded, flashing around toward her. "What have you been up to?"

But she didn't dare say anything and she didn't move.

"The world's turned upside down," Mama moaned, "children raising their voices to their parents, young against the old. The sky will rain blood." As she moaned, she rocked back and forth. "The cruelty of your own flesh and blood. If only I had known . . "

"Well, say something," Adrian said furiously as Willa hung in the doorway. "Don't just stand there like a lump."

"I want to go and play with Mary Anne," she blurted out before she knew what she was saying.

"What?" Adrian demanded. "Who is Mary Anne?"

Exposed, she had to tell the truth. "My friend. She lives down the alley," she said in a quick breath.

"Why, where'd you ever get that idea, child?" Mama said, looking at her, puzzled but not angry. She exchanged a glance with Adrian.

"She's making it all up," Adrian said. "No wonder she does so badly in school. She's always lost in a cloud."

"She is too my friend," Willa insisted. "She has a real father and mother."

"Which is more than I can claim," Adrian said, instead of asking her how she came to know Mary Anne.

Willa looked at Mama. She was big and fat, but she wasn't a tumor. She was just Mama.

"Oh Lord!" Mama said indignantly. "Which is worse—disrespect to the living or insulting the memory of the dead?"

"What was he when he was alive?" Adrian demanded. "That's the insult. A cheap drunk—a common bricklayer, who couldn't even support his family."

"He did his best. The world beat him down."

"The sot."

"You're inhuman."

"And you're a mess."

Willa breathed a sigh of relief. They had forgotten about Mary Anne.

"You always took up for him. Sat back and let him go through money like he knew what he was doing. I could have been somebody if I'd been given half a chance."

"You hold everything against me. Consider what I had to live through."

"You groveled in it. You . . ." His hand shot out as though he would grab her by the hair and tear it off the way Willa had once yanked the wig off her doll and left her bald.

"He did his best," Mama repeated lamely.

Willa couldn't remember her father, though she had two pictures of him in her head. When Mama talked about him, she saw a long-faced man with sad eyes and a puckered brow; but when her brother spoke, she turned away from two eyes like coals flashing fire and was stung by an evil-smelling breath.

"You live in the past," Mama said. "The dead past that can't be changed."

"And you can't see it," Adrian said. "You paint it up like a piece of calendar art."

Since they had forgotten about her, Willa went back on the porch to Clarise and Isabelle. She was going to take out their eyes and put them back in straight so they wouldn't be all cross-eyed and squinty.

For his vacation Adrian had gone back to the town where he'd been born, but he'd come home before it was time and was in a far worse temper than usual.

"It's all your fault," he yelled at Mama. "I couldn't walk anywhere in that town without people pointing at me and turning away. They refused to speak a word to me. And all for being Frank Clayborne's son and having you for my mother. They couldn't forget. I couldn't go back and hold up my head—all because of you." He turned away, flung himself into his study, and even slammed the door.

Her arm around Willa, Mama wiped her eyes and shook her

head. "There's not one word of truth in it," she said, "but he believes it like the gospel. Craziness—the stories he tells. He says I beat him every day when he was little—imagine! Says I put plates of food on the table but made him go hungry; says I rapped his knuckles with a ruler every time he reached for something to eat; claims I dressed him in rags; says I wanted to sell him to the gypsies that came through once; tells people he had to sneak off to go to school. To think I brought him into the world." She gave Willa a series of little light pats on the shoulder, but it was clear she wasn't thinking about her.

"He was different when he was little. We were poor then, and he did all kinds of things to help. He made crepe-paper flowers and sold them to the neighbors; raised pigeons and sold the squabs, and rabbits. When he was in high school, he wanted to be an actor. Used to stand with his face in the mirror practicing—bugging out his eyes, pulling down his mouth at the corners, stretching his grin from ear to ear—till his face was like a rubber mask and he could do anything with it. And I think he stretched it out of shape till it wouldn't go back, till something inside him was twisted, too."

Willa tried to imagine the rubber mask, but now Adrian's face with the yellowed skin tight against his cheekbones was more like varnished wood, despite the pendulous lobes of his ears and the nose that ended in a little globular drop as though it were starting to melt. His face looked cracked like old wood, but when he was angry his eyes blazed up. And when he yawned he looked as though he could swallow her. His teeth were very white and even.

"And yet," Mama went on, "strange things have happened to him. Said once he found a thousand dollars in the street. Said he was the escort of the Queen of Denmark when she came to visit in France. Said a movie star fell in love with him just from seeing him across the room. Said he owned a manuscript of poems by a great Irish poet and that these were stolen. Said he escaped death from a crazy man who swore he'd kill him because he looked like his brother. And all these things are true. And now I ask you, what's the sense in any of it?"

Willa wanted to know whether he'd be any different if all his lies were true and all the true things were lies.

Mama thought for a long time. "He would be neither better nor worse. For he believes in his own lies. No," she said, "not meaner, nor smarter, nor kinder. Nor easier to tell when he'd be any of these."

Sometimes he came in with a swagger like a soldier, holding himself so that his chest seemed to lead him into the room, and his head could have been fastened to his body by an iron spike instead of a neck. And sometimes he surprised them by leaping in front of them, dancing around them in a circle and laughing at their shocked silence. And often he was railing and cursing because nothing was right in the world. And now and then he was friendly and polite and spoke in a voice like other people. But you could never count on him for anything, for if he was kind, he could turn mean, and if he was angry, he could suddenly crack a joke.

"Now I ask you, what's the sense in any of it?" Mama said again. "Look at what's happened to me—look at this picture." She showed Willa a sepia-toned snapshot of a young girl with ringlets around her head and a face like a morning glory. "Now would you say I was the same as she? And what's become of the thoughts in my head then? Gone . . . Even when I try to remember. When I was little, I could run like the wind—and I thought if I flapped my arms I could fly. Now look at me." She tried to get up, heaving herself forward like a mountain looking for the faith to move it, then sinking back again. "Misery—there's a devil in the flesh, though nobody believes it any more."

"Are you going to sit there until you grow into that chair, or fix me something to eat?" Adrian said, as he reappeared from his study.

"You've put me in such a mood I don't care whether you eat or not," Mama said. "A lot you care for me . . . If you knew what I suffered in these legs and back . . ."

"Rationalizations. You talk yourself into it."

She looked at him. "I suffer."

"It's all in your head."

"Go away," Willa burst out suddenly.

"Don't you talk back to me," he said, advancing toward her with his hand raised.

She dodged behind Mama's chair.

"Let her be," Mama commanded. "She's only a child."

"This is the way you bring her up? What's she going to turn into, I ask you?"

"I've taught her to be a good child. To mind her manners and be clean and helpful—which is more than you do."

"You're not fit to be anybody's mother."

"Oh God—listen to him."

And they went on lashing each other, exposing each other's failings. As usual, Willa moved away toward the door to go and take refuge with Clarise and Isabelle. Maybe she would cut out their tongues. She opened and closed the door quietly, putting the thickness of wood between herself and the voices inside. She had not been playing long when she heard a little light tap at the front door. Though it was fogged with moisture, she thought she recognized who it was and wiped away a circle with her hand. It was Mary Anne, and for a moment the two of them stood and made faces at one another, laughing soundlessly, for Willa had put her finger to her lips for silence. Then she opened the door and beckoned her friend inside. "Come out and play with me," Mary Anne whispered, under the cover of the voices that clashed within.

Willa reached for her coat from the coat-tree and put on her boots. "Bet it's cold out," she said. The windows of the enclosed porch were so completely fogged she could not see out.

"But the snow's all sparkly and there are icicles to eat."

Willa remembered how she'd heard one crack and fall into the snow like a dagger. Suppose I pick it up, she thought, and smash the sun right in the eye.

Quietly they left the porch and stepped out into the snow. A little white curly-haired dog rejoiced when they appeared and tore off as fast as it could go. "Come on," cried Mary Anne, as she began to chase after the dog, taking great strides through the snow. Willa tried to follow, though she had to be the first to stop, quite out of breath. They walked along toward the open fields, where the evergreens were cut out against the sky. The snow was a field of diamonds. Willa jumped up and down.

"Listen, and I'll tell you what I did yesterday," said Mary Anne. "I went out to play in the snow all by myself. The grown-ups were all inside by the fire and didn't want to come out. But I came out with Tina, and we ran and ran till we were all out of breath. I chased her and she chased me. Then we began walking, and suddenly we came to a place where the snow just stopped and it was all green grass. Everywhere you looked there were trees all covered with peaches, yellow and ripe."

"I can see it," Willa said, for as Mary Anne told it she was there herself.

They made angels in the snow and built a snowman, and when Willa thought to look again, the sparkle was gone and the light was sinking. A crow flew overhead, cawing hoarsely, its shadow flickering across the snow. And she heard in it Adrian's voice.

She ran home then, fingers and toes now numb with cold. The cold outweighed her fear, though she knew what awaited her. But when she opened the door and went inside, the house announced its emptiness. The warm breath of heat made her skin tingle, and she heard the furnace making little clicking sounds. It was strange to be alone in the house, just herself in the space between the walls. And she had a strong sense of Mama's presence and Adrian's as separate and distinct from her.

The door to the study was open, but with Adrian gone something had been taken away, as in a problem in subtraction. She went inside and stood by the desk, right where she had stood before. She knew she wasn't supposed to be there, not even to look, for even with Adrian's absence the room belonged to him and spoke his disapproval. She picked up his pen, lifted up the top of the inkwell and dipped it in. And while the room waited in forbidding silence, she made one tiny scratch on an envelope, then another.

She heard the door flung open.

"Where can she be—oh, where can she be?"

"Wait'll I get my hands on her. She won't sit down for a week."

"She's gone—she's gone."

Horrified, she stood rooted to the spot. Then something gave way, and it didn't matter. She swept her arm across the desk and knocked over the inkwell. The inkwell shot to the floor, making a great spray on the rug. It was a creation. It looked like a feather drawn by the ink. It should have been white, but it was dark, and instead of lifting in flight it sank into the fleece. But she liked it, it was hers, there on the ground. And with a certain dark exultation, she knew her secret: even if the devil found her, she'd sneak down the alley to look for Mary Anne.

On the Eve of the Next Revolution

Their last day in Guanajuato, the three of them—Sol and his wife, Evelyn, and their son Steve—drove up to the statue of Pípila, who stands with raised torch on a hill above the city. They climbed the narrow stairs inside that go up to the head, discovered they could see nothing of the countryside, the panes looking out were so narrow and streaked, and came down again. Enthusiastically, Sol greeted the old caretaker in Spanish. Why not talk to everybody? was his philosophy, even though he knew his accent must be horrible. The discovery that he could call up his Spanish from thirty years back, that the knowledge had remained in his mind waiting, beyond the thick of the business of life, despite the passing of time, set him into eager conversation with perfect strangers. Perhaps being in a foreign country eased the usual constraints: he would never see these people again. As he talked and gestured, sudden lapses of vocabulary calling his hands into play, his wife and son looked on with a certain wonder, and possibly boredom, unable to follow what was going on. Though Steve had spent the summer in Mexico—they had come down to bring him back to Philadelphia and take a brief vacation themselves—and had studied Spanish at the university, he hung back on the edge with the self-consciousness of the young.

Sol put a couple of pesos into the old man's hand. "Well, we've seen it," he said, as they emerged into the air and started to walk to the wall encircling a space in front of the monument, from where it is possible to look out over the city. The close-walled houses descended the hill and ascended another beyond, with the winding streets along the narrow cleft between the hills dividing the city, church spires shooting up at intervals, and, as now, the bells clanging, pigeons being flung from the towers like scraps of paper. For a moment everything was lost in the clamor.

It was an amazing city, Sol thought. Sixteenth-century Spain had come to work the silver mines—then time might as well have stopped for three centuries. Only now the town seemed to have been goaded reluctantly into the twentieth century. Towers and wrought-iron balconies suggested the past. But cars and buses had to negotiate the narrow streets, along with burros bringing wood, delivering milk. At one point, a lightpost was bent at a crazy angle where a truck had hit it in an impossible attempt to get around a bus. But the past—it was impossible to stand there without being aware of it.

"They don't believe in flattering their heroes," Evelyn said, shading her eyes and looking up at the statue. He followed her gaze. The Indian knelt—a squat, muscular figure with a face that looked unfinished—and held up the torch. Yes, something of the brute, but something else, too, that can rise above fear to risk death. The suppressed animal, seizing his humanity, had rushed into history.

He read the inscription aloud, translating slowly: "Even now there are incendiaries who will inflame Guanajuato."

"I don't know," his son said, doubtfully. "The place seems pretty dead to me."

"Even with Ricardo and the others?"

"The bars are pretty jumping."

For the young, life was in the bars. But then, why not? Experience was to be seized from the moment. What did monuments and museums have to offer them? They held what was left after the fighting was over.

For it was a city of relics, and something oppressive hung in the air, like mourning. That day, they had come up on a little old couple, doll-like, dressed very formally in black, stately and withered. Sol had talked to them. A very sad city, they told him. In its history, yes, and for them, a nearer sorrow.

Their only child had died a week before her wedding. *Triste.* *Triste.* And did the Americans like Guanajuato? Beautiful, yes. But for them, a city of death. Had they been to see the mummies? the old couple wanted to know, and seemed oddly proud that the city could claim them as a tourist attraction, had preserved them in the underground tomb.

"You might be able to see the Alhóndiga from here," Sol said, moving to the wall. They stood, leaning on their elbows and gazing down into the jumble of roofs, the maze of streets. A murmur of street noises refined by distance reached them, accompanying sounds that were more distinct: the crowing of a cock, the barking of dogs, the braying of burros—an incredible noise—the shouts and cries of children at play. Another peal of bells gathered them in and sent out a flutter of wings from the tower. He liked the sounds of animals and people. For these few days he appreciated the slower pace.

"I think if I were a pigeon, I'd take up other quarters," Evelyn said. "They lead a harried life."

"Well, they're dumb enough for it."

"Isn't that it over there to the left?" Steve asked, pointing. "The long rectangle?"

"Must be."

Once a granary, now a museum. They had gone through it the other day, entering where Pípila, a flat rock on his back to keep off the musket fire, had scuttled up with his torch, fired the door, and touched off all Mexico. Inside—apocalyptic, violent in color—were murals of Indians in chains being whipped by the Spaniards; horses rearing and plunging in the confusion of battle; men wounded and dying. "You can see where they had the heads of the four leaders, on stakes at the corners," Sol said.

"A grisly touch," Evelyn said.

"For eleven years," he mused aloud. "Until Independence. Imagine." Hidalgo's had been one. But when you thought about it, a minor episode in the history of atrocity—hardly to be noticed in what had happened in the world since. At least there had been Hidalgo—his vision on the road. By the time it was over, it was hard to say which side had been capable of greater bestiality. Old systems died hard. It was costly, he thought, the birth of an ideal. But on the other hand. . . .

Steve, he saw, had wandered off toward a stand selling candy and soft drinks. Several ragged children immediately clustered around him, demanding nickels for sweets. In a moment Steve was talking to them, laughing, teasing them in Spanish. With kids he was at home. Sol turned back to the city. It drew him somehow, slowed him down, made him thoughtful and a bit depressed.

"We should get back soon," Evelyn said. "I've still got to buy something to give to Betty."

They were leaving in the morning. It would be his last night to talk to Felipe. How extraordinary it had been to find him! When Sol first walked into the posada, Felipe had looked at him and said, "I know you." Then they threw their arms around one another . . . A former comrade-in-arms had told Sol several years before that Felipe was in Mexico, but he did not really expect to find him. Or to be remembered.

They had been together in Spain. And to discover that the friendship begun in the camaraderie of war was still intact after a separation of so many years was, for Sol, deeply moving. Late in 1936, they had sailed together on the *Queen Mary* to Montpellier, on their way to save the Republic. There were a bunch of them, from all over. Felipe had come from California. On their arrival, they were to meet at a certain house; they would not set out until dark. Meanwhile, they were not to be seen together in clusters—they would be too conspicuous. As it was, everyone knew who they were and where they were going, including the gendarmes. They crossed the Pyrenees on foot.

He and Felipe recalled incidents, names. It all came flooding back, things he had scarcely thought of for years. Pancho? Ah, yes, who could forget Pancho—and the letter? How he always claimed he could read and write but would never carry a written message; it might fall into enemy hands. Then he got the letter. Everyone teased him to read it, but he had all kinds of excuses. But finally, in secret, he came to Felipe. To Pancho's astonishment, the letter was from an American woman who claimed to be in love with him. He showed the letter to everybody. . . Once in Barcelona—but who could forget?—he went up to Ibáñez and said, "On whose side are the descendants of Don Quixote fighting?" Sol remembered Ibáñez, too—who wore his sombrero so and held himself just so and walked with a glitter of silver. No man could have carried a heavier load of vanity. . . .

Their wives grew sleepy and finally went off to bed, leaving Felipe and Sol to their mescal and their war stories. Then after Sol was wounded . . . the last days of Barcelona . . . the retreat. At dawn they staggered off to bed. But Sol had been too excited to sleep: the past had come alive again.

He was like a spectator watching an old movie: it was strange to look at himself then, and now also to see Felipe, who still held a pure faith in the old ideals. Quite astonishing after so many years to see a man who burned with the same fire, spoke with the same words—"Bourgeois Decadence," "Elitism"—hated the Church and American capitalism with the same passion. Six years ago, his oldest son had gone off to join Castro's army, Felipe told him proudly, leaving behind a note for his father, "I want to fight for what I believe in." Now he was part of a guerrilla movement in South America. Felipe's younger daughter and her husband were organizing workers in Puebla. "The trouble here in Mexico," Felipe said, "is that the revolutionaries have gotten down from their horses and into their Cadillacs. The Church has gotten stronger. The poor are still poor."

Inherent in the nature of action, Sol remembered, from a book whose title he had forgotten, *is the degeneration of the idea.* "But at least there are schools in all the villages. Those are fairly recent, aren't they?" Painted brilliant orange, red, yellow, with the name of the teacher lettered boldly across the front, they were the only bright things he saw in the villages of wattle huts.

"Oh, there have been some improvements since I was a boy," Felipe admitted. "But everything is so slow . . . and such a trifle when so much is needed. Before one dies . . . one would like to see that it has made a difference."

Before one dies . . . To ask for some tangible proof that he hasn't wasted his time . . . Was that asking too much? Having helped make the world safe for democracy and watched that dream go the way of others and having demonstrated against Vietnam and for civil rights and watched the revolution of the sixties grind to a halt after its problematic effects, its inherent ironies, he had left the task of improving the world to those with clearer sight. His own vision had gone opaque with complexities, become clouded with ambiguity. Till finally the sphere of his action had shrunk to those things he could touch with his hands—and they were few and small enough.

When arthritis had slowed him down, he sold out his contracting business to his brother and retired. He kept himself busy. He landscaped the whole yard, he brought home piles of books from the library, and he tinkered down in a basement workshop: built wooden trains for his grandchildren, refinished furniture, repaired the irreparable.

Once he'd caught up with a truck taking battered musical instruments to the dump, and he'd gotten the driver to deliver them to his house—for a song, as he liked to say. He'd taken the horns of the trombones and some of the clarinets and made them into a fountain for the front lawn. It was a great thing to turn on the hose and see the water come whooshing out of them. Another time, in a salvage yard he gathered some odd parts from pieces of farm equipment and made a series of metal spiders that he hung in the trees on Halloween. The neighborhood kids thought they were terrific; the neighbors thought he was getting senile. Some days he didn't read the newspaper. And what did he think he was doing? he wondered.

Ultimately he had to admit his failure. Particularly with his kids. His daughter, such a bright thing when she was little, had ended up married to a dentist whose main activity seemed to be making money hand over fist, and both seemed perfectly satisfied with the good life in Shaker Heights in Cleveland. They were contemplating buying a Piper Cub—they already had a Porsche and a sailboat. His disappointment would be seen as ungenerous. But was one fighting, after all, for the right of the next generation to float in fat? Make the world safe for mediocrity? His older son was another case. Having been given the opportunity for a first-rate education, he'd dropped out of school his freshman year and seemed to be making a career of being a tennis bum and drifting—wanting, it appeared, nothing more than a good lay. And now there was Steve, his youngest, his Benjamin, whom he had anguished over perhaps more than the others, because Steve always seemed such a misery to himself and never quite fit anywhere.

"I've thinking about Steve," Evelyn said, quite as if her own train of thought had led her to speak just at the point where it converged with his.

"So have I," he said.

"You know, he'll be on his way to school only a few days after we get back."

"I know." Really, the time of his living under their roof had already ended.

"I don't want to be one of those worrying types that can't let go of their kids . . ."

He knew what she meant. She wished she could send him off eased of some of his self-doubt, able to enjoy himself a little.

Had he, Sol wondered, communicated to his son his own sense of uncertainty, his gathering skepticism? Things had gotten worse as he had grown older. For him, unlike Felipe, the old words had become stale, worn out, and he had found no new ones to exchange them for. He'd become suspicious of words—they had a way of turning into jargon, slogans, cant— rhetoric and pieties for the unthinking. The specter of a profound disillusionment stood beckoning before him. He'd just finished reading a biography of Simón Bolívar, who, near the end of his life, seeing the political situation he had helped to create, had asked the question, who are the three greatest fools in history? And had answered, Jesus Christ, Don Quixote, and myself. My God! Sol had thought at the time, and had to put the book down.

In another book he had underlined, *Life is unbearable for the man who does not always have an enthusiasm at hand.* Where was there a place for an old idealist, he wondered—a man who hadn't outworn his passion, at least not yet? Was there nothing left for him but to rot? At least he'd had his blaze of enthusiasm when he was young. So much for himself. But if you were young, if you were Steve and already torn with ambivalence . . . Doomed, he thought, to be old before your time.

"It's getting chilly," Evelyn said, putting on her sweater. "You want to go?"

"I think I'll walk back," he said, with sudden inspiration. "I'll see if Steve wants to go with me." And then he wondered what he would say to him, what he could offer him. He shrugged and let go of the imperative. Who needed advice? Let there be a few moments of companionship, the last they might have for a while.

He walked over to where Steve was sitting by himself near the end of the wall looking out over the city.

"You want to walk back with me?"

"Sure."

They accompanied Evelyn to the car, watched her back out and followed her into the road. Sol took his time, he wasn't in any hurry—not any more; the boy fell into his stride. He was a good-looking kid, Sol allowed himself—nearly six feet tall and well built. Decent, too. You wondered why the girls didn't come by the dozens. Too diffident, he thought—too unsure. And terrible with the small talk. He sighed.

"You have a good summer?" Sol asked him, an innocuous question.

"It was okay. It was hard to know how to act. Sometimes it's like you're Uncle Sam in person, sitting there making all their troubles. They look at you like that, as though you ought to feel guilty every minute. Rich American! . . . The girls were pretty."

"Ah."

"About all you could do was look, though. Good beer— terrible cigarettes. And nobody reads anything but politics.

They've got Mao by heart. Che Guevara. Long talks about Castro. Still a big hero. They kept asking me what I thought. I kept getting in trouble . . ."

"Not radical enough for them?"

"They thought I was a reactionary. I always put my foot in it. Like one night there was this argument—only right in the middle, one of the girls, from Ohio, I think, said that her underwear kept disappearing and what should she do about it? The maid refused to understand. She was down to her last pair of panties. Ricardo said it was a form of protest against Yankee imperialism."

"And what did you say?"

"I laughed. I said maybe the maid wasn't interested in politics—maybe she just liked the panties. I thought they were going to tear me apart. I was half-way joking."

"You have to be careful—it's like joking about religion."

"Anyway, I said I wasn't interested in politics. Didn't I care about oppressed workers, people starving? Of course, I said. Then we got into a fight—we were pretty drunk, anyway."

"Sounds familiar." They walked for a few moments in silence. "School will be good for you," Sol said, "—give you a chance to find your own ideas." Ideas, he thought. And then what?

"I just wish I knew what I wanted to do."

"It'll come," he said. "You can't rush things like that."

"It's just that some people know what they want to do. They're sure. Like Ricardo. He's going to be a doctor. Right now, he works as a volunteer ambulance driver—he's only sixteen. Every spare minute he's around the hospital."

"So?"

"A couple of weeks ago they were going to amputate some guy's leg. He was going to watch—wanted me to go with him. I didn't want to go, but he kept after me. They started sawing . . . I had to leave. It made me sick."

Sol shrugged. "And what does that prove?"

"He thought it was great, the whole thing."

Less sensitivity? Greater ability to hide it? More control,

more scientific objectivity? What could he offer, what comfort or assurance? In their pained bewilderment, it seemed as though they both held an end of the same stick. Perhaps it was easier, he thought, when a whole generation was fired by the same tasks and your convictions lay ready to hand. You could pick up a gun, join a demonstration. Now it was hard even to believe in yourself.

They were at a point of the road where it curved between two hills, the one to the east rising into a high barren ridge shaved off at the top. There were clouds above it, which had, as usual, darkened early in the afternoon, poured rain on the city for an hour and, though lightened, still hung there. On the nearer slope dozens of saplings had been planted, beginning just off the edge of the road and advancing up the hill. A stone marker indicated that they were part of a recent reforestation project.

"These hills used to be full of trees once," Sol commented, as he paused to scan the slope. "Felipe told me. Hard to believe, isn't it? They cut all the timber for the silver mines. Wonder what they are."

He and Steve climbed a little way up and examined the leaves of one. "I can't tell what kind it is. Must be pretty hardy for this soil, though."

A little breeze kicked up, caught the saplings, bent them slightly, stirring the leaves.

"It's a wonder anything'll grow here," Steve said. "Rocky as hell."

But as they turned to the road again, the landscape took on a momentary brilliance. The ridge beyond them, touched by the dying sun, was set ablaze, and the clouds above glowed with the color. The breeze had dropped; everything was quite still, as though awaiting a blessing. Then came a rustling, very faint at first, as though a light rain were beginning, and Sol looked up, expecting the first drops. But the rustling increased, and a flock of goats appeared from over the rise and flowed down the slope. Warm brown, sleek black, white, dappled, with sharp, delicate faces and slender legs, they passed, their small hoofs on the dust making the hush-hush of rain in the leaves. A boy walked barefoot alongside. He glanced up at the strangers, but gave them no sign.

Caught up in the experience, Sol stood as the flock passed and then watched it recede down the hill. There were no words, only a shiver down the spine. Steve had stood quietly beside him. Then in the same instant they turned, looked at each other, smiled. He had seen it, too, whatever it was.

Well, Sol thought, it won't be easy—was it ever?—and he had no wisdom to offer. In a sudden rush of tenderness, he put his arm around his son's shoulder. "Just think of this sometimes," he said, hardly knowing what he meant, but as though he had caught a sudden glimpse of some possibility of the imagination. You'll come out all right, he wanted to add, but it was enough perhaps that he merely thought it.

Sirens and Voices

After Herman Carmody and his wife, Bobbie, had made love with gratifying ardor and lain for a time in each other's arms and he had finally fallen into a profound sleep, Bobbie lay staring into the darkness. Two dogs kept her awake with their barking, rather like a man and a woman quarreling: blasts of deep resounding bark, followed by a monotonous, querulous yipping. Then the two intersected. Then one. Then the other. A car door slammed, probably Dee-Dee Dishinger coming home from her date: Bobbie could hear loud hilarious good-nights. The girl spent such a fortune on clothes one might have suspected her of having robbed a bank; but then she was cute, she ran with the country-club set. Her folks were poised on the thin edge of extravagance. The girl wanted nice things; Bobbie couldn't blame her.

(Trucks rumbling past on the highway; the blare of rock music from a car that left a wake of sound as it cruised toward Main Street.)

She wanted something, but she had no idea what it was. Chocolate cake, she thought, trying to seize hold of an image of what had created her longing. Devil's food cake with marshmallow icing. No, lemon pie with meringue three inches high. No, not that, either. What then?

(A police siren ripping the night to shreds.)

When the noise subsided, the mindless chirr of insects took over, and the night went grinding on like her own invention. It was as though a gang of foreign invaders had taken over the territory of her mind and set up some tacky, provisional government with endless factions among the various adventurers and riffraff that came wandering in, all warring for control. She remembered suddenly that Ricky had to have a cowboy hat for the school play. She mustn't forget to buy him one.

(Next to her a whimper like a faint cry from a distance: Herman in his sleep.)

But he did not wake up, not even for the commotion down the street. First the siren that came wailing ever closer till it ceased with a little burp right in the neighborhood. Then the ambulance.

Curious, grateful for any distraction from her hunger, Bobbie slipped out of bed and went to the window. She couldn't see anything. It was too dark, too far, and that part of the street was cut off by the old Catholic church that now belonged to the Faith Evangelical Methodists. She had to be content with speculation. Among the neighbors on this or the next block, it could have been accident, sickness, sudden death. But farther on, in the midst of a row of houses on the decline, in a derelict gray apartment house, it could have been a drunken brawl, a stabbing, or a domestic quarrel that included a gun.

She hung by the window, as though, simply by her waiting, the event would reveal itself to her. She thought of putting on her clothes and going down to the street, but it wouldn't look right if anybody she knew saw her. In the morning she'd find out from Ramona Tulloch, who knew everything worth knowing in the town, and who, if she didn't know herself, would find out from somebody who did.

She eased herself back into the four-poster bed and lay staring up at the canopy. The shadow beyond the foot of the bed was a bureau of burly walnut, and to the side, where she couldn't see it, stood a little dressing table that had made her cry out with delight when Herman brought it home from the auction. The house was quiet as she lay in her nest of shadows. Too quiet. Till shadow and quiet parted and she was struck by an idea. Of course, that's what they could do with the third floor. Ah! Herman: she put her mouth around the syllables. How she wanted to wake him. To tell him: she had discovered where they could put a jukebox. She had always wanted one.

"I don't know why we never thought of it," Bobbie said, as she poured herself a second cup of coffee. A bit ragged this morning. Hardly able to sleep once the idea had seized her.

The breakfast nook was a sunny, if nervous, little corner where the light kept dancing in and out, at times too much for her eyes. Herman, only half-awake himself, was trying to concentrate on what she was saying, the words tumbling into his ears like so many bubbles of sound.

"All this time that third floor has just been sitting there," she said. "And do you know what?" Her enthusiasm left him blinking. "We'll make it into a bar. Counters and stools on one side. A jukebox in the corner."

"A jukebox?" he said, looking up to where a great spider plant filled the window and, suddenly molten in the sun, subsided into the light. "A jukebox?"

"It'll be *fun*," she said. "Think when people come over— we can dance, really live it up. Our own private disco. And what about a player-piano?"

She amazed him, she'd always amazed him—the things she could come up with. Even now, when he thought there was not one more thing they could possibly do to the house. "But is there money?" he asked.

"Of course there's money," she said. "There's always money."

That too amazed him: he knew nothing about money. Bobbie always handled the finances. With accurate mind and efficient hand, she counted out the cash, paid the bills, knew how much they had spent and for what, while he floated somewhere above the hard edges of fact, somewhere below the insistence of her desires, the whisper of currency in between. That mere paper could do so much—amazing.

"Then, in the end wall," she went on, "a tank with tropical fish and plants—maybe the whole end wall."

The whole wall a fish tank: he was trying to imagine it. Just beyond him, from the cage in the corner, a great fluttering of green and blue wings, a squawking of budgerigars. A small touch of the exotic in the modern kitchen. And now for the fish kingdom.

"Are you listening?"

"Of course," he said, trying to clear away distractions. Was it his hearing, he wondered, or a certain sluggishness of mind that failed to keep up with the overwhelming fertility of her imagination? Though he was an interior decorator, his mind had been as chaste as a monk's cell till Bobbie got hold of it. Now it had come to resemble one of those huge auction barns, treasure piled next to trash, with hardly a space to walk through. A chuckle of astonishment came with his admiration for her. She had him stumped. She kept him wondering.

"I want all kinds," she insisted. "Angel fish and striped sergeant majors and piranhas and the little creatures that look like streetcars lit up at night."

"Would they get along?"

"Of course. You just have to keep them fed."

He considered. What if you forgot sometimes, or if not all of them ate those unappetizing thin wafers he'd fed to goldfish as a small boy, but had each a special diet that included each other? Or suppose you forgot to feed them, and instead of the endless indifference of circling fins there was the awakened eye of appetite?

"Don't you think it's a wonderful idea? Aren't you excited? And you know when I thought of it?"

"Where would we find a jukebox?" it occurred to him to ask.

"In Florida when we go. There's bound to be one there. You know when I thought of it?"

A jukebox from Florida. "No—when?"

"Last night—after the police cars came."

"When was that? I didn't hear any police cars."

"No," she said. "You were sound asleep."

The gleaming new meat counter in Slater's Market was a feature designed to convince the customers that here were the best meats in town at the highest possible prices. And indeed most of the matrons who were considered good credit bought them here and had them added to the bill with the other groceries. Slater's was the only store in town that still delivered.

The two women were standing in front of the meat counter, behind which Ellis Slater kept bobbing back and forth between the scales and the conversation, weighing out meat and trying to get things straight.

"Can you believe it?" Ramona Tulloch said. "Dead—just like that." She snapped her fingers. "I walk right by his place every day. Didn't occur to me I hadn't seen him since Tuesday. I'll take a pound of that ground round, Ellis."

"How strange," Bobbie Carmody said. "Last time I saw H. T. he was acting downright antisocial. Like he didn't want to talk to anybody. Herman's done a lot of worrying over him lately. He's going to take it hard."

"He the fellow that took the waitress home and held her for three hours and tried to rape her, only she escaped when he had to go to the toilet?"

"Of course not, Ellis—that was one of the teachers, and they fired him and he's left town for good."

"He's not the one that liked little boys, is he? Used to proposition them on the playground?"

"Whatever gave you that idea? He's the one the kids used to call 'Doc.' Was a counselor at the high school."

"Lived alone," Bobbie added, "in that little garage apartment on south Home."

"Sure, sure, I know who you mean now. Always came in and bought the same thing: two pork chops and a pint of coleslaw from the case. Always wanted to know if it was fresh."

"Is that today's liver? Give me a pound."

"Yeah, now I know," Ellis said, reaching for the pan of liver. "Doc. Good-looking fellow. Laughed a lot. Always alone except for the kids. You think he was . . . ?"

"All the kids loved him," Bobbie said. "Came around all the time to tell him their troubles."

"He once told me there'd been a great grief in his life, but he never would say what it was," Ramona Tulloch said.

"A man that old without a woman—" The butcher shook his head. "Now I don't call that natural."

"Remember how Eva Faye Brownley used to lie in wait for him as he walked home? Kept inviting him to dinner. Actually proposed to him."

"A sad case," Bobbie said. "Married to that brute for so long, then going to pieces when he died."

"Then there was the one that married the opera singer—can't think of her name—went off to California."

"Chased anything that wore pants."

Ellis laughed. He laid the package with the liver next to the others. "What did he die of, anyway?"

"They don't know yet. Just found him dead—had been dead three or four days. They're waiting on the coroner's report."

"That's what comes of being alone. It ain't healthy," Ellis said. "I should have asked him to come to our church."

Bobbie was wondering if H. T.'s drinking had finally done him in. Herman had tried to talk some sense into him. "Herman and I were in high school with him," she said.

"I'll bet there's a woman in it somewhere," the butcher insisted. "See if I'm right."

On Valentine's Day, Bobbie remembered, all the girls pinned hearts on H. T.'s door. He used to joke about it. "See all my girls—they're in love with me."

"Ellis, you have a suspicious mind," Ramona said. "Now give me some of that sausage."

Bobbie thought she caught his thumb on the scale. But he whisked the paper away too quickly for her to be sure. She'd been buying his meat for years.

"Well, there's an explanation for everything," the butcher said. "It's all in knowing what it is."

"Well, it's all bound to come out in the papers," Ramona said.

And what would they know then? Bobbie wondered. And what difference would it make?

As Herman turned down Home Street toward his place of business, he noticed an unusual activity, as of wasps or hornets moving in and out of their hive, and located the source and target of movement as the doorway of the little garage apartment where H. T. Morgan lived—Ole Doc, as the kids fondly called him. The coroner was coming down the steps in Herman's direction: Lyman Cleaver, a tall, hearty, horsefaced man with tobacco-stained teeth. Along with being coroner, he ran the local funeral parlor, a brick building on the corner of Main and South, where he frequently stood in the doorway, thumbs looped in his vest, greeting people as they passed by—out of an inexhaustible sociability. He knew everybody, above ground and below.

"'Morning, Herman," he said. "You heard the news? Terrible thing. Friend of yours, wasn't he—H. T.?"

"Good God, what's happened?"

Cleaver shook his head, grimaced as if he might be genuinely puzzled. "Been dead for three days at least. Didn't show up at school. Didn't answer the phone or the door. Finally had to have the sheriff break in the door and there he was—"

"I can't believe it. What could have happened?"

The coroner, thumbs looped in his vest, leaning back, one knee slightly bent, was ready with an answer: "Looks to me like he electrocuted himself. The way he was laying across the bed, foot dangling next to a bunch of cords. That's the way I figure it."

"Why, that's terrible. Poor old H. T." He hardly knew what to say. He struck out blindly. "You don't suppose he got sick—maybe had a heart attack?"

"Of course, we can't tell anything till they run the lab reports," the coroner said. "And we can't rule out the possibility of foul play."

"But that's preposterous," Herman said. "Who'd want to kill H. T.?"

"You never can tell."

Maybe. Maybe there's always someone around who'd like to knock you off. More likely, Herman thought, H. T. had staggered into the cords. Probably blind drunk. Could he have wanted it? A chilling thought. But the way H. T. was drinking lately you could almost believe . . . He tried to remember back to a time when things might have gone differently, when he might have turned him around. He'd tried hard enough. Like talking to the air. Everything he said H. T. treated like a joke, just shrugged it off. But it was all bluff, you could tell. Once, he'd let down the facade: had ended an evening of drinking down at the Elks' Club by bursting into tears, had sat there weeping and hiccuping and shaking his head as though over some unfathomable and terrible fact. There was an embarrassed hush among the fellows at the bar. A couple of them came over, patted him on the back, tried to joke him out of it. Then they left him alone: crying drunk, that's all. It could happen. So they went back to their own drinking, and the hubbub rose around them again.

"Is he really dead?"

"What do you think I said?" the coroner responded, looking at Herman as though he didn't have good sense. "Guess I know a dead man when I see one."

But that wasn't what he meant.

"Well, got to get back," the coroner said. "How come you never drop by the Elks anymore? They got some great new flicks."

If he said they bored him, that he had a wife at home he found far more interesting, they'd never believe him. "Don't have the time," he said.

The coroner clapped him on the shoulder. "You got to make time, old buddy. Gotta relax, enjoy. Don't take it too hard," he advised. "Can't let things get you down. Come on over tonight and I'll buy you a drink." The yellow teeth came forward in a grin to put off the doleful.

"Thanks—some other time," Herman said. My God, he thought, H. T.'s gone, and tried to imagine the world continuing without him.

At the same time that the *Evening Star Bulletin* was coming off the press and being counted into bundles for the newsboys to deliver, with a picture of H. T. (Doc) Morgan smiling across the front page—deceased, cause of death as yet undetermined—Herman was ringing the doorbell at a home on the east side of town, in the Green Addition. Doctor's house:

game room, wine cellar, swimming pool, tennis courts. Doctor Bannister. Divorced and remarried. New wife wanted the house completely redecorated.

He hadn't wanted to come, but he made himself keep the appointment: unfair to impose your troubles on your customers.

The woman who answered the door and stood smiling as though she herself were the climax of an extraordinary joke, looked familiar.

"Don't you recognize me, Herman?" she said. "You must have read about the wedding."

"Eloise Moaks!" he said, startled into memory. He never read the newspaper. If he'd heard her name, it hadn't registered. "What are you doing here? I thought you were a nun."

"I was," she said. "Only now it's Eloise Bannister. But do come in. It's wonderful to see you again."

She was dressed as though a bridge club might be arriving any moment: gold earrings, gold necklace, many gold bracelets on her wrists, sending off little gleams and jangles as she stood in a white dress of a rough, yet clinging, sentiment. (*Eloise, dear, you look lovely,* would say the lady with the blue-rinse hair, as she patted her on the arm.) The aura of her perfume rose evocatively around her.

"I know it's a shock," she said. "But suddenly it came to me that it wasn't the life-style I wanted. Deep inside, I had other aims and goals. Until I met Carleton I never really found myself."

(*Found herself?—found herself a man*—that was what he heard Bobbie saying with a derisive laugh. *The wonder is she didn't find one in high school.*)

"It was our work that brought us together," Eloise went on, "with those poor children in the home. Poor lost lambs. He was so lonely then, Carleton was—just lost, poor darling. He used to talk and talk—Lela never really understood him. One thing led to another, and here we are." She opened her arms, making Herman a presentation of her new life. "But tell me about yourself."

There wasn't much to tell. He'd started off in cushions and

drapes at Sears after turning down a chance in underwear, then worked his way up to carpets. After Bobbie's father had died and the business was sold, Bobbie had set him up as an interior decorator.

"In high school I had the biggest crush on you," Eloise announced. "You wouldn't even look in my direction."

His face flushed.

"What did you ever see in Bobbie, anyway?"

Whew, what a question! Trying to corner him.

"She has nice teeth," he said, trying for escape. Something simple, even simpleminded.

"Nice what?"

"Nice teeth. I always admired her smile."

"Pooh," she said. She wasn't going to let him get away with it. "Is that why you married her?"

Her irony made him perspire. What a question! Why did anybody get married? You saw a doorway open and you thought, ah love—go for it! If you discovered reasons . . . it was afterwards.

"Silly me," she said. "It's all water under the bridge."

"Nice place you've got here," he said, lamely.

"It will be," she said, meaningfully, "when I get through with it. I want it all in white: white carpet, white furniture, white walls, white drapes. Just for a note of contrast, I've thought of getting a Siamese cat. But now that I think of it, an ocelot would be more dramatic."

"Definitely more dramatic," Herman said, as he reached into his jacket pocket for his glasses, took out his notebook.

"Oh, there's time for all that," she said. "But first, how about a little drinkey-poo?"

Drinkey-poo? Had he heard right? "No, I—"

"Come on now, don't be so stuffy. For old time's sake."

She went to the bar at the end of the living room and poured out two generous sloshes of Scotch. "I take mine on the rocks," she said, handing him a glass. Perhaps it was a challenge.

He took a tentative sip, rather like a high-school girl trying out her first whiskey sour. He didn't like to drink during working hours—he had a low tolerance for alcohol. But it was good Scotch and went smoothly down.

"Sit by me," she said, patting the spot beside her on the sofa. He sat down as if on command. "There—that's more relaxed, isn't it?"

It was better—only worse. Given a strong invitation by her perfume, something inside him began to waver and float. He didn't trust himself. He had the feeling she knew his susceptibilities.

"You know," she said, looking into his eyes in a way that unnerved him, "the years have done well by you. You look— mature."

"Well, I—" He shrugged. Words eluded him.

"Even distinguished," she said. "And I . . . don't I . . . don't you . . . ?"

She was waiting. "Mature," he said. "Very mature."

She frowned: clearly he had disappointed her.

"You're lovely," he said. It was what she wanted to hear, but was it what he wanted to say? He had just enough presence of mind to say, "I think you should tell me what you want me to do."

"That's easy," she said, getting up immediately. "Come in here."

He stood up uncertainly.

"I want to start in the bedroom," she said. "With the interior."

The doorbell rang. They had come to measure for storm windows.

Pre-cocious interruptus, Herman thought. Beads of sweat broke out on his forehead.

Since it was the end of the month, Bobbie worked late that afternoon. A bookkeeper for her father's advertising firm, she had stayed on when the two younger partners took over. Ordinarily, she was home by the time the children returned from school. Now she was in a rush. She had to drop off their daughter, Gloria, to spend the night with a girl friend, and buy a cowboy hat for Ricky before the store closed. When Herman came in, he found Bobbie in the kitchen cooking spaghetti. He could tell she was in a bad mood.

"I tell you," she said, "if I'd only known what I know now, things would sure be different. They made it sound like they were losing their shirts. I'm positive that lawyer did some fancy finagling. And I'll bet you Dempsey Stringfellow made it worth his while. Now they're making a mint. They think I don't know what the score is—that I'm too dumb to figure things out."

"But we're doing all right, aren't we?" Herman said mildly.

For some reason, he remembered the way Stringfellow had looked at Bobbie during the festivities of the last office Christmas party. "Maybe you should quit," he said.

"Don't be silly. The point is, fair is fair."

(Stringfellow's eye had taken the plunge of her neckline, as he stood poised, on the point of spearing a smoked oyster, and continued to roam appreciatively in the area.)

"I still think you should quit," Herman said. "We can get by."

"It's been a day," she said, ignoring him, setting plates of spaghetti in front of them, then sitting down. "I suppose you heard the news."

"About H. T.? Lyman Cleaver told me. I still can't believe it." He laid down his fork.

"And to die like that—all alone."

"They think he might have electrocuted himself. And if he'd been drunk . . . senseless, senseless."

"You think that's what happened?"

"I don't know."

"Do you think he could have . . . ?" She looked at him and paused. It was in both their minds.

"I don't know. He was drinking like a fool. I haven't gone around there for weeks. I just couldn't stand it. Every time I went by, there he was, smashed out of his mind with a room full of kids pouring out their hearts. I wonder if that's why he drank."

"He was their god—they all came to him."

"Only maybe underneath . . ." He paused. Ole Doc. With a smile and a joke for everyone. Except that one night when he'd seen the curtain drawn back . . . He didn't want to think about it—how when you drew back the curtain and there was nothing left you could call rational . . . .

"I don't know," Herman said. "Maybe it was just an accident." Did that make things any better?

"I always thought he had a mother complex," Bobbie said, "the way he ran from women."

"But it was his father that ruined him."

"Only his sister was the favorite in the family."

"And his mother's death tore him up."

"And then his father's remarriage."

"Plus he hated his stepmother."

"And she spoiled her own children to death. Just blind partiality."

"And what does it all prove?" he asked suddenly.

"She was a witch."

"His father was a bully."

"And H. T. was always the clown, the buffoon."

"That was his act."

"Well, it didn't fool me. You could see he was a marshmallow," Bobbie said.

Herman saw the fires of hell. Marshmallow? A blackened cinder.

"The world's a tough place. You've got to be tough. Sometimes I just want to strike out where it would do the most good. Stringfellow, for instance. Seems like every time I turn around, he's looking over my shoulder."

"I wish you'd quit."

"I can't."

"Why not? We're doing all right, aren't we?"

"You know," she said, with sudden inspiration, "why don't we go to Florida early this year—and stay a month?"

"Is there money?"

"Of course," she said. "There's always money. Sometimes," she said wistfully, "I think I'd just like to be a beachcomber and live on the beach." She smiled. "Wouldn't that be lovely?"

Just then their son came tearing into the room. "Hey, Dad, you want to see my cowboy hat?"

"Hey, that's nifty. Come here, though—the price tag's still

on." Herman took it off, looked at it. "$49.50," he said. "Isn't that a bit expensive for a cowboy hat?"

"I read it wrong," she said. "I thought it was $4.95 till I got to the cash register. I didn't want to bother going back, standing in line again."

"She bought one for Charlie and Mike, too."

"They came with us," she said. "I'd have hated to disappoint them."

That night Herman was unable to sleep. Bobbie had taken a sleeping pill and was lying inert beside him. But he was restless, on edge. Whenever he was about to drop off, Eloise Moaks or H. T. broke in with their obscene gestures of love and death. Like sirens, their voices wailed in his ears, blending with the sirens outside that broke the night apart. He got up with a thirst for something cold to drink and a desire to listen to Mozart.

First he thought he'd try a sandwich—entice the juices of his brain down to his stomach, so to speak, to help him sleep. He stole out of bed and down the stairs. In the kitchen the canary-colored walls leapt out at him, while the orange and brown curtains framed panels of darkness. As he spread peanut butter on toast, the fluorescent lights that made the bronze stove and refrigerator glow eerily blue seemed to hold him under surveillance, as though he'd been caught in a forbidden act. Unnerved, he looked around suddenly, a stranger in his own house.

With the comfort of peanut butter, he walked into the living room to stand under the softer, more archaic light of Tiffany lampshades. He felt a sense of pride when he walked into the living room, the dining room, the den, which reflected his work, had brought his real talents into play: stripping paint from trim and wainscoting, restoring the fine old carved oak woodwork, reviving the newel posts of the staircase. Then selecting the furnishings: the marble-top tables, the mahogany chest, the brocaded sofa, the great oak dining table. Some of his happiest moments had gone into making the house the showplace of the neighborhood, especially in laying out the garden.

When he and Bobbie were first married, then poor and struggling, they'd bought one of the older houses people were neglecting. A beauty, a monument of the old aristocracy in the town. They'd put every cent into fixing it up. He paused to look at the intricate carving of fruits and flowers around the beveled glass in the dining room, the play of color from the crystals of the chandelier, the design of the parquet floor. It was good, all of it.

First, they had done the downstairs, then the bedrooms. By that time, they had more money; the children were old enough to choose their own decor, and the house seemed to take off beyond him. Gloria's room was a collage of posters of rock stars plastered over black walls, with strobe lights exploding in volleys of color while rock music blared and beat. Ricky's room was the inside of a spaceship, with panels of knobs on the walls for various games, and green Martians on the ceiling. In a large plastic bubble he could retreat to watch television.

Just when everything had been finished, it was Bobbie's whim to turn one little unused space into a beauty room. They had spent hours at auctions so that they could reconstruct the interior of a beauty salon of the twenties, with hair dryers, mirrors, curling irons, and copies of old fashion magazines.

Astonishing what the house had become under his hands, as though a powerful agency had taken him over and moved through him. Nor was it finished. Now the third floor: bar, jukebox, fish tank. He had a sudden image of Bobbie swallowing the whole state of California, moved by every wild and gathering impulse, to the point where one day she'd simply walk into the sky—a pink sky, flaring with rockets. But if that's what she wanted, then somehow he wanted it, too. To make her happy—that's all he'd ever wanted to do. Just make her happy.

A sudden impulse on the way back up to bed made him pause at the door that led to the third floor. Pulling it open, he flicked on the light and climbed the stairs. The attic boards creaked under his feet as he surveyed the space. Choking from the dust, he went to the window and forced it open. For a moment he stood looking down into the garden, into the shadowy beds. In the delicately scented night he caught the breath of roses and honeysuckle. How many hours he'd spent digging and watering, tending and admiring the flowers. A sudden happiness recalled itself, and for a moment he could almost hear the moonlight trembling in the grass. He waited as though something might gather itself out of the light, out of the silence . . . .

A shuffle behind him. "Are you up here, Dad?" his son wanted to know. He turned to the boy, who was still blinking with sleep. "I had a bad dream," he said. "I thought someone was coming to get me from outer space."

No sirens announced the arrival of Dempsey Stringfellow and the firm's lawyer, George Meeker: merely a knock at the door of the blue house and the two of them emphatically, if quietly, on the front porch, in their three-piece suits, carrying their briefcases.

"Forgive us for disturbing you," Stringfellow said, always the gentleman. "But Bobbie is home, I believe. We have some business to discuss with her."

"Of course," Herman said, a little surprised by the sudden materialization of those he knew only from the office Christmas party. He invited them to come in and wait. Bobbie was in the shower.

The men rose as she descended the stairs, as though to pay her homage—Meeker, a groundhog of a man, who carried his shadow with him like a folded handkerchief; Stringfellow, lean and deeply tanned, with the kind of blond hair that takes in streaks of gray and seems never quite one or the other, and the good-looking-boy face of a man used to being handsome and perfectly aware of his charm.

"Ah, Dempsey, George," she said. "What an unexpected surprise. But do sit down. Can I give you a drink?"

"How very kind," Dempsey said. "Perhaps another time."

"Then perhaps you won't mind if I have one," Bobbie said. "Herman?"

"No, no, thank you," he said, puzzled, for Bobbie never

drank in the middle of the day. He searched their faces for some clue as to their business. But until she made her drink and came to rest in the Queen Anne chair by the fireplace, Stringfellow kept up the expected casual chitchat.

Then, as though on signal, the lawyer began to speak. "During the last audit of our books," he began, "the accountant discovered a discrepancy, at first a careless error in the Laskey account. But then—" He coughed delicately and cleared his throat. "On further investigation, similar discrepancies appeared in some of the other accounts."

"What are you trying to say, George?" Bobbie demanded. "Dempsey, what is all this?"

Stringfellow, head back, tips of his fingers together, as if to dive or pray, unperturbed, said, "I think we're just stating a few facts. May we continue?"

Herman looked at his wife, who frowned and took a sip of her drink.

With a glance at his employer, a shift in his position, Meeker continued: "Owing to the frequency of the discrepancies," he said, "it appeared advisable to investigate further, to reexamine records of past years."

Although Bobbie had sat back in her chair in an attitude of ease, she seemed to give off little waves of heat. "What are you saying?" she flung at him.

"That you have embezzled well over a hundred and fifty thousand dollars from the firm within the past six years," Stringfellow said. "Receipts not recorded, checks to phony accounts—it's all here," he said, patting the briefcase.

"It's a lie!" Herman protested. "A frame-up and a lie."

Ignoring him, Stringfellow turned to Bobbie. "You're a clever woman," he said, in a tone that did not begrudge her her talents. "You almost pulled it off." He allowed her to savor that possibility, then snatched it away. "But for one really glaring error, it might have gone on for many more years. But the proof we have should stand up in any court, and though we could prosecute, we thought we might try something more—civilized." He appeared to be handing her a life-preserver. Would she accept or not?

"What are you suggesting?" she asked. "That I allow myself to be intimidated by all this nonsense?"

"I am suggesting," he went on patiently, "that the firm would gain nothing by letting you rot in prison—and there is something owing to the man who gave me my start—" He did not appear to notice the glare this drew from Bobbie. "But if we can recover certain assets—" He was looking around: "House, furnishings, new car."

"Indeed," she said, standing up. "And do you think for one moment I'd submit to your blackmail? What unconscionable greed. It's not enough for you to swindle me at the beginning . . ."

Stringfellow and the lawyer had risen as well as Herman, who was debating whether he should throw them out of the house.

"No doubt, you'll want time to think things over. I'd advise you not to leave town. Your choice is whether you want to go to court and face conviction or, as I said, something a bit more civilized. I thought for the sake of your family, you might want to avoid unpleasantness."

"How kind of you," she said.

They left then. She waited until they left the porch, then turned back into the room. For a moment she and Herman stared at one another across the space.

"Is it true?" Herman said, aghast.

"Do you believe them?" she said, with a smile.

"Of course not."

"And if it were true," she asked, "would you hate me?"

"What a question."

"If you didn't, then it would be only to get even with me. Torment me."

"What?" He was at a loss, trapped in a riddle. "Even if you did it, it wouldn't matter. We have each other." The formula sounded desperately trite.

"Well, it doesn't matter, anyway," she said, "because they're not going to get away with it."

"Is it true?" he asked again. Somehow he had to know.

She smiled as if her mind were elsewhere.

"But why then?" he said, assuming the worst. "We were doing all right."

"Is that all you can think of?" She broke away from him, moved to the window. Savagely she plucked the dead leaves from one of the begonias. "Daddy worked himself to the bone for years, and those jerks come along and make a killing . . ."

"They gave you your share."

"That's what you think. They knew the value of those assets—way beyond what they told me. And I was so innocent—God! Thinking they were all so broken up over Daddy, and how they were trying to do their best for his little girl. I was such a *fool*. Stringfellow knew. He had his finger on everything. As soon as they paid me off, suddenly there were all those accounts I knew nothing about. Only *he* could get away with it."

"But you knew they'd find out sooner or later."

"Is that what makes them right, me wrong?"

He was stumped.

"And why should they have?" she said, reasonably. "There are millions of things people never find out—or don't find out till years later. And all the time they've been thinking they had the truth."

"Yes, but—"

"They don't even know yet how H. T. died," she threw in. "Maybe they never will. Suppose somebody killed him—had sat around planning it for years. There're lots of perfect crimes, lots of unsolved murders."

"But *you'd* know," he said, already tremulous with the discovery that that was the whole point.

"Of course," she said. "Suppose I did do it," she said, not granting him anything, "why, I'd walk into that office every day thinking, *I know something you don't know.* I'd smile to myself every time I looked at them. I'd *enjoy* it. And all this," she said, "the results—I'd enjoy that, too."

She meant it. That was clear to him. And she must have done it, though . . . .

"But don't think they'll get away with it," she said. "They're just trying to pull a fast one."

He was completely bewildered.

"They just think they've found something out," she said. Mystified.

The coroner was making a list of all those who'd known H. T. Morgan and who had been with him at any time during the days just before his death. The question was, who had seen him last? There was a brief flurry of excitement when one of the high-school girls admitted to having visited him in his apartment the last day he was seen alive. They'd drunk a beer together and passed a joint back and forth. There were brief rumors about whether or not she would be charged, but with what it was not exactly clear.

"Nothing," the coroner was saying to Herman. "Liver in excellent shape, considering the way he was sloshing it down. No sign of heart attack or stroke. Wasn't electrocuted. Health was good." He shook his head. "There's nothing to go on. It has me stumped."

"Maybe he just died," Herman said.

"People don't just die," the coroner said. "There's a cause. There's a reason."

Herman shook his head. He didn't know how to put it. "Maybe he couldn't live."

"That's no explanation," the coroner said, exasperatedly.

"But what if you don't have a cause?"

"Then nobody'd ever die," he said, throwing up his hands.

They would, though, Herman thought, for death was in the world. It didn't matter what you called it. For a moment, he toyed with possibilities: ultimate combustion, spontaneous entropy, power failure, thanotropism.

"Don't you see," Cleaver went on, making one last effort to break through such thickheaded perversity, "that won't do at all. The public won't stand for it. They've got to have facts." He gave a sigh, perhaps of weariness. "Is there any other name you can give, anybody else who knew him?"

Herman shook his head. At least with a perfect crime, you knew it was a crime. He knew nothing.

Maybe all you needed were a few facts on your side, Bobbie thought, but sometimes even that didn't do the trick. And when so much was at stake, you might as well play the game for all you were worth. She was excited, a little scared. A bit of a flutter in her stomach, a catch in her breathing. The slightest noise, magnified by the quiet that had settled over the house, sent a tremor through her. She strained her ears for some sound from the sleepers upstairs: Herman in the four-poster bed, Gloria among her rock stars, Ricky on his way to Mars. They would not wake; no, they mustn't wake. "I'll come to bed soon," she had assured Herman. "I'm too edgy right now. I couldn't possibly sleep. I'll relax with a drink." She wouldn't let him stay up to keep her company. Better if she were alone.

Bobbie had kept telling him not to worry, that everything would be all right. But the past few days he'd scarcely been able to eat. Food sat on his stomach like cannon shot. His mind went spiraling, then came back to the same place: everything would be all right—it was all one great mistake. But how could he be sure? He wanted to believe her. Or did he simply want hers to be the truth? Oh, what did one live by anyway? Did you ever really know whether lies were true or true things lies? And when you awoke . . . if you ever did . . . .

She sat on the sofa in a peignoir, a magazine on her lap, turning pages: money-saving tips for meals, the latest foolproof diet, the most recent article on the Kennedys, ten ways to improve your sex life—it all passed before her eyes without interest or effect. Would she really be able to pull it off? Was it really going to happen? She had a sense of the possible, of the tremendous latent power that could make things go one way or another. If you could only get on top of it, make it go your way.

She heard a car approach and continue a little way down the block. She glanced at her watch: nearly one-thirty. She went to the window, drew the curtain back slightly and peered out.

Then she glided to the door, turned the knob ever so gently and opened the door to let him in. He came inside, followed her as she motioned him into the little den off the living room. She closed the door behind them. That much at least was done.

If she wasn't guilty, how could he account for their accusations? Was Stringfellow so depraved he had to devour anyone who strayed across his path? But if she were . . . Then it would all come apart, the whole untidy bundle of their family life spilling out—into the newspapers, into the streets, to be taken up by friends and strangers. Newspapers that would broadcast the facts . . . for all who cared to tear them apart and chew them up for motives and scrape the bones. And what would they know when they got all done? Or he?

"Well," Dempsey Stringfellow said, smiling at her with a certain benign satisfaction. "This is cozy. Can we talk?"

"Everybody's upstairs," she said. "Asleep."

"Good," he said. "I think there are things both of us want to say."

"You know what this has done to me—" she said. "I'd do anything to keep from hurting Herman or the kids. It's all so—overwhelming." The word came breathily, and she paused, for the sake of magnitude, trying to get his mind to accept it. "The thought of losing the house, everything."

"Of course," he said. "I realize how much of a blow it is for you." His tone suggested that he was a man not without sympathy. Meanwhile, he was fingering a silver lighter on the antique carpenter's bench Herman had made into a coffee table.

"But that's not what I mean," she said, touching his arm. She waited for him to look at her. She had to have his full attention. She opened her hand. "What would I be without all of this?"

He moved toward her then, and drawing her close to him, ran his hand along the flimsy material of her peignoir, to her shoulder, above her breast. There he paused. "You'd still be—" He allowed his eyes, a curve of the lip to express what mere words could not.

"What do you mean?" she demanded.

"—Desirable."

"Does that matter?" she said, lifting her eyes. This was not her only card, but since it seemed a good time to play it, why not?

"You know how I've always felt about you."

"Not exactly. And I'm not sure you understand."

"Of course I understand—how you've tried not to waste yourself—in this life, in this town. And I've admired you—don't think I haven't. Your pizzazz. You've got it. And you've used it to take what you can get."

"But to hold onto it," she said with a smile. "That's the main thing." Then, so as not to sound too deadly serious, she said archly, ". . . If possible."

"And do you believe in possibility?" he asked, pressing her close to him, insinuating his hand between them.

"Of course," she said, raising her eyes. There was indeed something here she could make use of, not to be tossed off lightly. Maybe you could even dignify it by the notion of a philosophy.

Now when he came home in the evenings and stood before the blue house it seemed scarcely real: it might vanish in an instant, go up in a puff of smoke. Don't worry, Bobbie had said. They don't know what they're talking about. But something had happened—nothing was the same. When he walked by H. T.'s little garage apartment he saw a young couple moving in. As though H. T. had never lived there, had never been. And what had happened to all the years they'd known each other . . . failed to know each other? The newspaper had reported finally that, according to the findings of the coroner, H. T. Morgan had been electrocuted by a faulty cord. So much for the public peace. Not that it made any difference.

"I love Herman," she said, drawing back, removing his hand, for it was distracting her. She had to keep a clear head.

"Of course," he said, drawing her toward him again. "It would be terrible if you hated him."

She saw he could be generous, he was so much above Herman.

"I don't want to hurt him," she said, looking up into his eyes, into the face that would never grow old. "I don't want to die," she said. "I don't want to be thrown into a corner like an empty beer can." She hoped it was a good line, not too rehearsed. She tried to gauge his reaction.

"Who does?" he said with a little smile.

"And do you know," she said, "I've always felt a kind of bond between us—that we wanted more than just . . . oh, you know what I mean."

"Yes," he said, smiling down at her, gently pushing aside a stray lock of hair on her forehead. "It's all a game, but you may as well have a little fun with it."

"So you can understand why, when you arranged for all the payments to come to you in cash so that you could beat the IRS, that I made my own copies of the receipts and noted carefully the names of the clients—just in case."

She thought she saw him blink at that.

"Oh, you did that, did you?"

"Yes," she said. "And don't you think it might be bad for business if, say, the Nelson brothers and I. J. Peters were accused of complicity?"

He was having a terrible dream: the house was filled with strangers and all the furniture was on the lawn being auctioned off. Somebody had bought the four-poster bed, and the little bureau of burly walnut was going, going . . . He was looking everywhere in the crowd for Bobbie—walking up to people, asking where she'd gone, but no one could tell him. He sat up, a cry ringing in his ears, but whether it was his own voice that had awakened him or a siren off in the distance he was unable to tell. He shook his head, trying to shake off the reality of the dream.

"So it's all been a terrible mistake," she said with a smile.

"And things will go on as usual—nothing to mar the surface after all."

Though his face had gone red for a moment, he'd recovered his composure. "You scheming little bitch," he said, with almost a chuckle of admiration escaping from his anger.

"And where did I learn it?" she said archly.

She was conceding him something in that, perhaps enough for him to allow her her triumph with good grace. At any rate, he smiled and reaching out, seized her by the wrist and drew her toward him. What did he have to lose? But what did she have to gain? Even as she caught the scent of his Pour Lui, she resisted gently. She still had a few things to figure out—there was the future to consider. For the moment, maybe she should just hang on to what she had, to what had taken so much of her life—before the old restlessness came down on her again.

Black Hole

That afternoon when they were together, it struck Ruth that she and her mother could have been any two women joined by a cup of coffee. As if their relationship had moved up or down a notch. Her mother had her shoes off, her legs folded on the couch beside her. The brilliance of sun through the pear tree outside showed up the streaks of dirt on the windows at the same time it gave a brief glory to the confusion of leaf and bloom of the houseplants Helen had crowded together on the sills. Helen still wore the bandanna she tied round her head when she worked in the garden or went out to feed the chickens and gather eggs, or to inspect the rabbits in their pens. She was a handsome woman still, but her significance lay elsewhere. In her expression, in the way she sat, in everything she did, something was asserted that made her arresting. To Ruth, it was rather disconcerting that they might have been simply two acquaintances drinking coffee, as though this woman had never been her mother, had never been married to her father, but was reverting back or moving forward to something else that wasn't altogether clear, perhaps even to herself.

"Mother," she wanted to say, while she waited for the woman at the drop-leaf table in the corner to find an article she wanted Ruth to read. Wanted to see her raise her head and respond, become familiar to her in the old way. For some reason, she thought of one of John's patients, a cantankerous old woman they had been rather laughing over, who had spent fifty years as a salesclerk forced to smile and be pleasant to people all day long. And now she figured it was her turn—to be nasty to everyone . . . .

Was that how it was? You earned the right to some hidden part, some shadowy thing that lurked around the edges of all you had been called upon to do? Looking around, at the windows that hadn't been washed in God knows how long, at the stacks of books and magazines that either represented her mother's latest enthusiasm or were simply the piling-up of things not yet put away or thrown away, she had to ask, How did it happen? What was it that gave to her mother's life this particular drift? Here in her little house on the edge of town, the furniture worn to her own particular shape and purposes, alone most of the time with her chickens and rabbits, which she killed and dressed and sold; alone, except for the visits to and from Ruth and her family—what had she become?

Her habit of going to the tavern in the evening—that was new. To the tavern frequented by workingmen and strangers traveling through. She'd never been one for going out, not even to the hotel bar where she might have gone, let alone to the tavern.

How did it happen?

That was the question she had first asked herself about what her mother's life had become. Then it had become the specific question for the whole bizarre situation. As she drove home, it was *the* question. She couldn't fathom it.

How did it happen?

By the moon—an orange moon. He put a hand on my arm. Just a touch, but the place burned . . . And he held me, by a chain. Oh, you couldn't see it.

She had looked at Helen: her mother. Was she mad? That was her first thought.

I laid my head on his chest. I felt his breath on my neck.

The words repeated themselves obsessively, like a tune she couldn't get rid of. When it suddenly occurred to her to look at the speedometer, she found herself driving over the speed limit and slowed down.

Mother, you're— But she couldn't say it. Perhaps that was

part of the reason she was angry. Quite furious, in fact. The way her mother went maundering on. Beyond the bounds of all reason. If not crazy, then, yes—infatuated. Isn't that what the word meant? But how could she, a woman—hardly an adolescent schoolgirl? And going on in the language of that infatuation. Not even looking at Ruth. Her eyes off in the distance.

I'm only trying to explain.

Explain. As if that explained anything. Craziness. Infatuation. Or more crudely, had she been drunk? After all these years, the hidden part a penchant for drinking? She talked as if she were drunk still.

But, Mother, it isn't the first time you've ever had a drink. And what made her mother go to that sort of place to do her drinking? A place where she'd never have been seen years ago. Could she really have been drunk? She'd never known Helen to put herself in that condition. Oh, a few drinks; maybe to the point of being a bit silly or garrulous. Nor was it the first time she'd ever laid eyes on a man. *And you say a total stranger?*

Yes, I'd had a few drinks, her mother admitted, with an impatient gesture, dismissing them. She paused and frowned and turned her head as though help might come from some other direction, not impossibly from the sunlit streaks on the windows. When she spoke, she might have been speaking, not to Ruth at all, but to someone totally outside the conversation. *The light so filled me I swam like a fish. And when he took me, I went with him. All the way. So taken up I left myself behind.*

Utterly absurd. Ruth could hardly concentrate on her driving. She was thinking: she couldn't even remember the man's face. The face of her lover! Absurd. All her mother knew afterward was that she awakened in the front seat of her car. No doubt somewhat the worse for wear. And the man was gone—probably never to give Helen another thought, never to wonder what might have been the consequences of that simple act in the dark.

Mother, do be serious. When she found herself saying it, she couldn't help thinking: it's all turned around. I'm the mother and she's the child. *She,* the exasperated parent.

You don't have to have a baby simply for having— Taken one too many. Let down the controls. Been foolish. *These days they can take care of that.*

Yes, I know—

And you can see a counselor. I mean, it was practically a rape.

Well, I wouldn't have called it that.

And then her mother had smiled as though she were back in that moment, still savoring the pleasure of it. It was all Ruth could do to sit there, she was so nearly ready to burst. And now, she tried to remember, tried to go back. When was it something in her own life would have had any correspondence: her first crush? The currents and bursts of confused emotion that had caught her during adolescence, when she didn't know what she was becoming? The anger, the terrible loneliness, the hunger for something she couldn't define. Perhaps at no time had she ever been so isolated in herself. Was that it? And could she have clothed her sensations in words, perhaps they would have sounded as mad as this. For afterward, even the intensity of what she had called love, even the feelings called up by her pregnancies, the arrival of her children, had been so surrounded by plan and pattern that these too seemed only the familiar, the expectable.

But that afternoon she couldn't think. And then as now, she felt imposed upon in some unique impossible way. As though no one had the right to exert such a demand.

What would you call it? She had to force herself to be reasonable. *Anyway . . . you can get help.*

Yes, I realize.

Besides the danger.

Yes, the danger—

Mother, you're not paying attention. It was infuriating beyond anything, the way the conversation kept landing in a drift of inconclusiveness. At the moment only one fact could be stated with certainty: now at the age of fifty-three, her mother was pregnant by an unknown man and, in violation of reason and sanity, intended to have the baby.

In many ways it seemed unfair that John, after having spent a day at a clinic where most of his patients were alcoholics trying to change the pattern of their lives, should have to come home to a crisis of the sort Ruth was going to face him with. As she tried to gather herself together so that she could talk to John when he came home later that evening (no, it wasn't going to make any sense, but she was going to have to give it a try), it occurred to Ruth that it must have been even more difficult for her mother to break the news to her. For she knew that Ruth held a certain stature in the community. John was highly regarded as a doctor. He served on the hospital board and was invited to speak at various meetings throughout the state. Helen could imagine how ridiculous Ruth would feel trying to explain all of this to an overworked, decent, sensible man.

It was, to say the least, a chore. But Ruth was no snob. If anything, she admired her husband for a kind of dedication that went beyond any consideration of class or income or family. He worked too hard, she knew that. He didn't get enough sleep and at times looked haggard. He did too much, and did it with largesse. He genuinely liked people.

Besides, even though she'd thought Helen was wasting herself there on the edge of town when she might have married again, Ruth had never apologized for her mother. Not when people said to her, "We never see Helen in church anymore," or "Where's your mother keeping herself these days?" And she had no intention of neglecting or abandoning her now. But that didn't mean she wouldn't try to talk some sense into her if she could—before she made herself and everybody else miserable.

What did her mother want a child for, anyway? At this time of her life? She couldn't imagine Helen making one last desperate fling after lost youth. That didn't seem to be her style, either, walking around as she did with a bandanna on her head, a trowel in hand or a basket of eggs.

Why would she want to go through it all again? She already had two perfectly available grandchildren, whom she was fond of and who adored her almost as much as her chickens and rabbits. And what would happen if such a child appeared on the scene? Certain ugly pictures came to mind—her kids being ridiculed at school, the child itself being rejected. And she could see the gray-haired old woman her mother would be in a few years, with the child by the hand, saying in response to people's friendly, if intrusive questions, "No, she's my daughter, actually." Much to the delight of the vulgar.

Going off on a tangent, she wondered, how would they all be related, anyway? Uncles, cousins? Was there a word existing for such a family connection?

And subtly, if calculatedly, she had tried to hint something of all this, now so much more logically organized in her mind, to Helen.

I never wanted to cause anybody pain. But it is my life.

That was the most she could get out of her. Of the risks to herself she faced, Helen seemed quite aware. She'd merely shrugged when Ruth had posed that question. There was nothing further to say. *At least talk to John*, Ruth had pleaded before she left. *Do that much for yourself, if not for me.*

Now to her husband, she said, "You're not going to believe this, but my very own mother, and your mother-in-law, Helen, is going to have a baby, fathered by a total stranger."

Before he could say anything, she continued. "Yes, I know. I can't really believe it myself. It's just so bizarre." Should she take hold of that particular strand, follow where it might lead—to some of those horrible pits of aberration and disease: hormones, cells gone wild, tumors pressing on the brain? Senility? She said simply, "Do you suppose it's her time of life?"

"I've known some strange things to happen," her husband said.

He did not offer to go on, perhaps in deference to her feelings. She remembered one terrible case in which the woman hadn't really survived the change of life, but had gone entirely out of her mind, ending in an asylum—incurable. But none of that seemed quite to apply.

"I won't even try to tell you how bizarre it was, the way she described the whole thing. I mean, it happened out there at the Tanyika Inn—God knows why she ever went there. If it were someone else, you'd say she was drunk out of her mind and got laid—Oh, it's terrible to be saying such things. But to her, it's as though she's had some kind of tremendous— experience."

She was ready to weep, simply from the pressure of events and the dizzying circle of her thoughts. John put his arms around her.

She kept on, not allowing him to speak, as though she were trying to prove to him that she had turned over every stone, exhausted all logic—as though to prove she hadn't betrayed herself by some collaboration of sympathy. "And I tried to remind her how dangerous it would be at her age, but it's like talking to—someone who isn't there."

"And of course the chances for abnormality . . ." he said, taking her up.

"We didn't even go into that. I just don't know what to do. The whole thing is just . . . You will talk to her, won't you?"

He looked at her tenderly, gave a little shrug. "You mean to put behind it the weight of my profession. From what you say, I'm not sure that will have any force. But then, I'm fond of Helen. I'd hate to see her come to any harm."

"I know. I knew that's how you'd feel—and the way I feel, too."

"But if you really think there's something wrong mentally, physically—that maybe she should see a psychiatrist . . ."

She was glad he had said it. "I really wish she would. Something has to be wrong. But how can I say that to her? I don't know— Maybe living like that, she's just gone peculiar." Now she was weeping. "I simply can't understand. Really, I do think she must be crazy."

He didn't say anything at that point. She felt the pressure of his hand on her arm, his way of telling her he knew how upset she was. Finally, gently, he said, "But you're not thinking of really raising the question of your mother's sanity. We've seen Helen all the time. She's always acted like a perfectly sensible . . ."

"No, of course not. I mean . . . No, I couldn't do that. Only . . ."

"I admit this isn't what I'd have expected, not what I'd have thought Helen had it in her to do." He shook his head. "I thought I was beyond being surprised by anything— I will talk to her, though, try to put the case as seriously as possible."

"Thank you," she said, wiping her eyes. She was grateful to him. She felt exhausted of ideas, and it seemed she'd just go round with the same old ones without getting a fresh stock. In fact, she said again what she'd been saying over and over to herself: "But why would she even want a child at her age? That's what gets me—" She thought of more. "Considering all she went through to get the two of us raised, then having Frank killed in a car wreck. I thought she'd never get over it."

"Can she even support one?" he asked.

"I don't know that it's crossed her mind," she said. "I'm sure her eggs and rabbits and what-not don't bring her more than pin money. She's always refused to take anything from us. How does she think she can feed and clothe a child?"

"Or provide a future, some kind of opportunity?"

"How long does she think she's going to live—?" Her anger was beginning to mount again. "You can't live as though there's no one else in the world. There are other people, other lives. It's totally irresponsible," she said, really angry now. "Even immoral. Bringing a child into the world like that. What if she gets sick and can't take care of it—why, she might not even live to see it grown." She took out a cigarette to calm her nerves. John was much opposed to her smoking, but at the moment she needed a cigarette. "I hope to God you can bring her to her senses."

Though some people hold a certain awe for doctor and lawyer, for the authority of the scientist, John always felt that his mother-in-law, though she respected him, apparently liked him, followed certain of his cases with interest when he spoke of them, treated him rather as a man going about his business. He did not ask for more. They were at ease with one another.

And now he was, with real discomfort, he had to admit, going to speak to her, out of his concern, which was certainly real and personal, but which carried with it the authority of his profession. It was as though he were pulling rank on her: *Don't do it. It's bad for you, and the weight of evidence is against you.* And yet what did his training and knowledge mean if he couldn't speak in the light of them?

He found her out in back, this time in boots, hat, and ancient mackinaw hosing down the yard. He suspected that if the pregnancy continued, she would be doing the same tasks until the final days before delivery. She was that independent—to the point of folly.

"Well, John," she said, greeting him. "I know why you're here," she said, apparently ready to make it as easy as possible for him. "Come on inside. I'll be with you in a minute."

He waited till she had turned off the hose and followed her inside, then sat down in the faded armchair in a room that impressed him as no different from usual. Her furniture, most of which very likely went back as far as her marriage, was battered and faded, though still serviceable. Except for the stacks of magazines on the table and the straight-backed chair, her house was neat, even comfortable. She came in when she had taken off her things.

"I know better than to try to change your mind once you've made it up . . ." he began.

"I'm glad to hear you say that, John," she said, sitting opposite him.

"But," he continued, "I want to be sure you understand how serious all this is."

"Yes, I know I'm an old woman. It's a wonder nature herself didn't take care of all this a few years back." She smiled. "A grievous oversight."

"It doesn't mean you still can't do something," he said. "I know some women have an instinct that's deeply offended and particularly if they have a religious background . . ."

"No, no, it's nothing of that. I'm not resisting because of any moral grounds. And knowing my age and everything against it, maybe I would have, only . . ."

She paused, seemed to fall into reverie. He wasn't sure she would continue. "Only what?" he prompted her.

"It's like this," she said. "You go on all your life doing things the way you suppose they ought to be done. And for all I know, maybe that's the way it should be. I'm confused myself. But then something happens. It's like you fall into a black hole, a place where you've never been before. And you can't tell anybody what happened because you don't have the words for it, not even for yourself. Only the experience. Maybe it's like one of those black holes they've discovered in the universe."

"But, Helen," he protested at this misapplication of science, "black holes are created by dead stars that have left the universe . . ."

"Well, I know that," she said, "but maybe that's not all. Maybe they'll go on to discover something else. Maybe there's something down there inside, just waiting to come out."

He wanted to get back to the real issue, but he was momentarily snagged by this image of her confusion. It was a wild surmise, a haphazard statement of faith. He sat there as a scientist. And it was true that behind his efforts was the implicit motive of the certitude of light: the cause found, the cure discovered, the unknown given a name. And yet . . . it was rather abstract, this notion. Meanwhile, the elusive symptom, the ineffectual treatment, the relative states of sickness and health. And in spite of all, the buried mistakes.

"But the child," he said, wanting to come back to something specific. "What's that got to do with it?"

"Everything," she said, a strange light in her eyes.

He was mystified.

"Don't you see," she said, with an urgency that made her

voice strange in his ears. "Whatever happened to me, when I fell in—if you don't mind my putting it that way—well, there's only the child . . . There's only . . ." She seemed to have trouble saying what she meant. "Otherwise, it would be lost."

"But, Helen," he protested, quite mystified as to how to win through to her. "You have no idea what this child will be, or what kind of danger to you to have it. Why, it could be—"

"Oh, I know all that. Retarded, twisted. Yes, monstrous. Yes, I know." She sat thoughtfully. "That would be horrible, of course. And if I knew that for a certainty, I wouldn't take the risk. But there's a chance, you see—maybe for something else. For something that till now never existed."

The tenuous hope— He was surprised to find her clinging to it. "I hope you're right," he said, suddenly tired. He'd spent a lifetime trying to deal not only with nature's mistakes, but the mistakes imposed upon her by the human. There were times when he thought, the only way to do anything here would be to go back and start all over again. No, he had seen too much to suggest that anyone deliberately put himself in the way of suffering.

There appeared to be nothing more to say. "Well, take care of yourself," he said, getting up to leave. "At least give yourself the best possible chance."

He still had his afternoon clinic ahead of him. Obviously she was going to do it, give birth to the child that would give her the living image of whatever her experience had been. And they would be waiting, fearfully, nervously, to see what the child would be.

Land of Promise

The end of the day: time to close. She had been on her feet all day and her legs ached. And she had gotten practically zilch out of Angie, the little girl she was training for behind the counter—slow as molasses and no head for even simple arithmetic. She blamed the schools. Help was always a worry—they loafed or they pilfered or they couldn't make change. The bright ones stole and the dummies stood around. She sighed. At least the sales items had gone well.

Fanny Wasserman counted up the cash, made out the bank deposit, and closed the safe. Moving along the cases of scarves and costume jewelry, she turned out the lights as she went. She took one last look around at the tables of marked-down goods and the racks of dresses that hung ghostlike along the walls, as though to reassure herself they'd all be there when she got back, then turned out the last lights, shut the door, and locked up.

Outside, dust mingled with the twilight. Just up the street the city hall was dark, where during the day old men and the local police lounged out in front, spitting on the sidewalk. The lights of the Buffalo Bar were on. Later, the bar would be loud with cowhands and Mexican miners, and being Saturday night there was sure to be at least one fistfight and a knifing to bring in the police from next door. Later, too, would be the high-school kids tearing down the street in their cars, circling the flagpole at the end, and tearing back again. But now, as Fanny crossed the street, it was quiet, the sidewalks deserted but for a couple of early drunks shuffling homeward.

Tired . . . tired, she thought, as she started up the hill.

When Ben was in the store with her, he drove her home each evening—it was good to have a son. But now she walked rather than take a taxi—it was an expense. She grew breathless. The town was nearly all hills, and the one that rose up near the center of town was long and steep. In the mountains it was hard to breathe, the air was so thin. Why couldn't she have lived in a town where the streets lay flat? There were other places—Florida, California. The years had burdened her—all their burdens she carried in her flesh.

At the top of the hill she turned up a dirt street to a narrow two-story brick house that stood on a little hill of its own. The iron fence leaned at an angle, and the yard was all weeds. Who could get anything to grow? She'd given up years ago her efforts to call forth a little grass. Opening the gate, she sent the grasshoppers left and right as she walked up to the porch and climbed the steps.

The house was dark, and she knew that Moe was gone. He'd been planning to go, if not this week, the next. A note would be waiting for her on the kitchen table. She had a piece of calf's liver to cook for him if he'd been home. Now she'd have to eat it herself two nights in a row. Let him go, if that was what he wanted. In a few days, he would turn up with a gray stubble of beard and a sackful of rocks that he would take down to the assayer's office or else polish up for gemstones. He was a strange man, her husband. The years had accustomed her to his strangeness but had given her no clue to fathom it. She sighed, full of weariness. "Going off in the bush like a young kid." It was too much to think about and useless to blame him.

Three small trout were frying to a delicate brown in a skillet over the fire, sending out a smell that made him roaring hungry. The sun was just at the top of the bluff on the other side of the river, light glinting through the pines. The fire felt good to him. The coolness leapt up from the stream just as the sun set, and the day was over, even though the light lasted a long time.

He sat on the ground watching the river until it was time to turn the fish. He always started out his forays into the hills with a night on the river fishing, and he stopped on the way home, too. Farther up, on one of the creeks, he sometimes panned for gold after a rain. But this time he would drive his truck up into the Black Range, leave it with a rancher he knew, and take a horse out into the hills to prospect for manganese.

When the fish were done, he lifted them out onto a tin plate and deftly removed the backbone, leaving the delicate white meat practically boneless. He'd fished for crappies and catfish in the Rio Grande down below Socorro, but the trout pleased him the most. He liked looking for them in the deep little pools along the mountain streams, liked the way they flashed out of the water and fought on the hook: a crystallization of the stream itself, quick and silvery, as it tumbled down over the rocks.

When he had eaten, he drank the coffee he had boiled, black and bitter, but to his taste. He watched the sky and the light in the water and the smoke curling away from the fire.

Fanny would be home by now. He saw her at the kitchen table eating by herself, a woman with heavy arms and breasts, a heavy tired body. He caught a glimpse of her face, with its expression dark and moved, as though the flesh, ample though it was, could barely conceal some deep-seated grief. For her, he knew, the years had meant one long betrayal—he, the betrayer.

He shifted uneasily where he sat. Her image blocked the view, and he could no longer watch the river and the setting sun and let his thoughts flow into them. It was always like that: human things intervened and made it hard for him to find his way back to the feelings that led him there in the first place. When he was alone, he was always trying to put together a justification of himself: "Well, you see, it was like this . . ." And the shades of his wife and sons stood by as audience; behind them, the handful of Jews who lived in the town, and behind them, the town itself. Over the years, little gleams and lights had come to him, flickering here and there but lighting up no certainty. And each time, he had to start over. "Well, you see . . ." And now he would think a long time and lie awake a long time before his thoughts would let go of him and sleep gather them up and set them aside. It was always such a struggle.

She did not feel like eating, she was too tired to fix supper. She would let the liver go for another night. Some bread, a piece of cheese—it didn't matter what she ate. She made herself a pot of tea and sat at the kitchen table drinking tea and watching the sky darken. It was dark in the kitchen, but for a long time she did not get up. She watched the lights come on in the houses on the hills across town as the mountains beyond merged with the dusk.

What would Moe be eating for his supper? Beans cold from the can—for sometimes he didn't even bother to heat them up. Fish he caught from the river and cleaned with his knife. Then he would make his bed on the hard ground and lie down to sleep in the midst of the vast and lonely places of the desert, on mountains with nothing but rock and cactus, tracked by coyotes and mountain lions. She thought of rattlesnakes and scorpions, and a chill ran down her spine. She had never grown used to the things that crawled and moved in the grass. Even the lizards that appeared suddenly, a quick movement here or there, startled her. Ugly things, they sent up the expectation of harm. At the worst, she imagined Moe carried off by a flash flood or dying of thirst in some desolate spot, buzzards circling overhead, bones picked clean and bleaching in the sun. She'd seen cattle skulls whitening on the land, with eye sockets for the wind to blow through.

She got up and turned the light on all the alien things. Whenever Moe went off, her thoughts hovered over him, a sick man, though that had been years ago. They'd come West because he was a sick man, and she still thought of him that way.

She'd never trusted the land. It was a hard land, and from the very beginning she'd never felt at home. She'd lived there like an alien, her feelings having been given their shape by a single image, the ground of her unsettled life.

The train stopped, and the four of them, she and Moe and the two boys, were swept onto the station platform, the wind swirling dust around them, and left there like so many pieces of unclaimed baggage. For a few minutes they stood waiting for their belongings. Some boxes and trunks were taken off, an elderly couple put on. Then the train pulled out of the station, gathered speed, and before it disappeared, briefly marked the distance like the stroke of a pencil. The station-master went inside, and they were alone, sunlight wavering before their eyes, the dust coating their teeth with grit. Before them, the land unfolded into vastness, the pure sweep of distance broken by a solitary ranch house and the column of telephone poles disappearing into the desert. On the horizon was the faint imprint of distant peaks. That was all. As they stood on the platform looking outward, it seemed to Fanny that they would be drawn into the distance themselves and swallowed up like particles of dust. . . .

"Moe, you are crazy," she said aloud, as she went into the living room to the television, where faces and voices lived. How could he lie down and sleep when so many things waited in the darkness?

He lay under a great cottonwood, the trunk bathed in moon-light. It was a white streamer of light, the solid trunk flowing upward, and his eye followed it to where the branches netted the stars and caught the moon in a shattering embrace. He lay there, trying to put together the broken pieces of moon. He had come to be reminded of this, a gift, a blessing—the moon in the trees, light bathing the trunk, flowing across the water. And if he let go, the moon would take him back again, down through the years, as though to the bottom of a well, as he remembered how it happened that he was here now.

It had taken those months in the hospital so long ago to make space for the beginning. He'd lain there in the hospital that had been converted from an old army outpost on the Butterfield Trail, built originally to protect the settlers from the Indians. He'd gone out to New Mexico when they sent veterans there to recover from tuberculosis or else to wait to die. He'd waited, too, but whether for life or death he had no idea.

It had been difficult lying there, letting time flow over and past him. He'd been full of guilt because the burden of his sickness lay upon Fanny, who had to work and take care of the kids. He worried about Fanny and the boys and how far his money would go. He worried about the future, about whether he could find a living and what he would do. And he thought of the long days he'd spent on the road as a salesman of boys' shirts, and of the long nights on the outskirts of towns. He brooded over how hard it was to get new accounts and how business had fallen off; his stomach had been in a continual knot.

Then he worried because Fanny came to him full of trouble: they were among strangers in a strange place. Anna Silberman had done this to her, and Rosie Katz had done that. And the boys were made fun of in school and the town was . . . She could hardly find words for the town.

Yes, the town. "Look in that direction, Fanny," he'd said. They were at the railroad station, trying to get their bearings. "You can't see it yet, but it's behind those hills."

And there it was: a cluster of houses at the bottom of a valley, the streets rising and falling till they were lost in the hills in dirt footpaths alongside the adobe huts, whose roofs went up the mountain like steps. The last lap of their journey had been by bus, for the train did not go there. They had climbed the mountains in a series of hairpin turns that made Fanny close her eyes, she was so terrified they would fall from the edge of the cliffs to their death below. Finally they descended and bumped down through the main street, a double row of beaten-up old storefronts, broken here and there by the vulgar intrusion of something new. The sidewalks were built up a couple of feet above the street. After the first rain they discovered why: the adjoining streets, more like alleys, were unpaved, cut by gullies that carried little streams of water across the main street to wash into a ditch below. He watched her sinking beneath the weight of her fatigue and the disappointment when her eye was caught by a sign: "Silberman's Department Store—Since 1880."

"Look, Moe," she cried, pressing his arm. "There are Jews even here."

Yes, he thought, as he lay under the cottonwood, for her, that had been a discovery. And who were the Jews there? The Katzes, who'd had a dance studio in California and now a clothing store where the Mexicans came to buy cheap. And Anna Silberman, who was in her sixties and stood on her feet all day because her department store was her only life, though it was killing her. And Gertie Silberman, who was as rich as Solomon but who wouldn't spend a dime. And Jack Silberman, who owned half the town. And Abe Frank, who sold used cars and gambled his money. He'd known them all before, had found them everywhere he'd ever been, and lived with them and drunk with them and cracked jokes with them and done business with them and heard their troubles. And it never occurred to him that he wouldn't always be doing exactly the same.

But in the hospital everything changed. Time had flowed over and past him, and he found himself outside it. As he sat there looking out across the land, something happened to him. Something had moved within him, though he couldn't say what it was—had winked at him from beyond the mountains, suggesting possibility. Who were the Jews here? Who were the Jews anywhere? The Jews had poured out of Europe to make a home in the desert. Before the turn of the century, his father had come to America to escape conscription into the Prussian army. And now he, his son, was here in New Mexico.

When he came out of the hospital, he had shed his troubles from the past and his worries over the future like a skin that no longer fit, and he felt strangely naked and alone. The land was before him: height, space, distance. He wanted to know the land, to know it like a woman, in all its forces and moods and gifts and exactions. And he would have to give himself to it, not take first. This he knew, as if by instinct. But then what? He had no idea.

And did he know now? he wondered, as he looked for a

moment's calm in the moonlight. After so many years of wandering the land. Was it for this that the Jews had spent forty years in the wilderness?

Once again he had deserted her. She would have to turn on the television for the sound of a human voice—to talk about aspirin. She should listen, she had a big enough headache.

He did not live in the world, Fanny thought bitterly— where the rent was to be paid and the tax notices came and there had been sons to be raised and given a stake in the future.

All he cared about was rocks. Rocks. Rocks in his head. And what had ever come of his passion for rocks?

"Fanny, I tell you there's treasure still waiting. Think what they've found here. Silver—tons of it. Overnight a boom town. Copper, manganese. In the hills are riches."

He should be the one to find them. A little gold dust he had taken out of Turkey Creek after a rain. So live on that and let dreams fill an empty belly. She'd had it up to here with his notions. Or the time he'd come upon a vein of feldspar. The excitement then. One of the mining companies bought the rights. And they were to wait for the royalties to come pouring in. But the company never mined the vein—it would cost too much—and probably never would. Now he brought in agates and malachite and obsidian and quartz crystals and fossils that he sold to rock collectors and jewelry makers, while she stood on her feet all day and tried to keep everything going. And he was going to make them rich. She had to laugh.

If only he could have seen things her way. They would have had the store, he and she together. He knew the clothing business—he hardly knew anything else. And from her uncle she'd had a little money. But would he listen?

He was sick to death of that kind of life. "And what do you get for it? You work your *tokus* off and for what?"

"To live? What else?"

"And that's life?"

She'd been so upset she could hardly speak. But what do

you say to a man who has come out of the hospital? And she thought of how he used to drive himself—for her, for the boys. Then she had to make him slow down, take it easy. Then he had no time. When he came home, he was worn out. He saved money, tried to invest it, lost it, made another start. He worked hard to provide, make a decent future. She loved him for his labor and tried to reward him with a nice home, always clean, a good meal on the table, and she there to greet him, fresh and cheerful no matter what.

So what did he want to do? He had looked off in the distance as though for inspiration to come to him out of the blue. "A piece of land . . ." he said reflectively. "They raise cattle here." He spoke of Jacob with his flocks and herds.

"What are you talking?" She had a sudden image of him as a cowboy on a horse. She wanted to laugh. Better not to argue or irritate him. She thought, I will do what is necessary and when his head is clear, he'll see things my way.

She had rented the building and ordered the stock and opened for business. The boys worked hard at their subjects in school and read good books from the library and got paper routes, and when they were older they helped her out in the store on Saturdays and during the summer.

But none of this made any impression. He slipped away from their view: no more a husband or a father or a man who belonged anywhere. Outfitting himself with some Levi's and a pair of hiking boots, he went off into the hills.

Now as he lay under the cottonwood in the moonlight, it seemed to him that he had come to this spot at this moment, if not to be delivered of a burden, at least to know why he had borne it. So many years and for what? He felt sick at heart. As his eye climbed the tree like a ladder to the moon, he did not know whether anything might descend, whether any benediction might flow in the darkness.

If he had to give an account of himself, he could say that he had not wandered the hills in hopes of making a killing, though he spoke to Fanny of riches that were there. He would have been glad to make a living, if such had been in his power.

But even that he had let go of along with everything else. First he had read geology books to learn to recognize rock formations and the presence of the major ores. Then he read history and legend. He learned how the explorers came, men hungry for wealth and power, adventurous men who took risks and shed blood; other men with a mission and a duty to save the souls of the vanquished. He read of Coronado looking for the Seven Cities of Cíbola with their golden roofs. He read of lost mines and buried treasure. Then he set out to search for whatever he could find.

He panned a little gold dust and brought back samples of manganese and feldspar. He learned the impress of the geological ages upon the faces of the rock and brought back fossils from the time the land had been an inland sea. He came to know the stones that could be polished into gems and brought these back, too. But these were all his riches.

He saw how the arroyos were made by the force of the rain sweeping down from the hills and how the wind had carved the faces of rock. He hiked the rocky ground among prickly pear and yucca and ocotillo and saw their brief bloom in the spring. He watched the mountain meadows come to life with the spring rains and the grass turn brown with the sun and the drought. He had seen coyote and bobcat and deer, quail and wild turkey, rattlesnake and lizard, tarantula and scorpion. He had fished in the streams and camped among the pines. He'd been drenched by rain and parched by sun and chilled by the cold on the desert at night. And that was all.

He had come back to the town with sacks of rocks that were assayed and labeled and given their worth. And he had walked the dirt streets and the paved streets of the town, bought tamales from the Mexican kids selling them on the streets, and climbed the hills among the adobes until he stood overlooking the town like an explorer who has suddenly come upon a strange race of people. He had done all this.

And now as he lay under the cottonwood, while the moon freed itself from the branches and moved higher in the sky, suddenly he knew that this was his gift, or perhaps his curse: to wander the land and never have a home.

How could she have forgotten to look in the mailbox? Ah, she didn't know where her mind was. She heaved herself up from the sofa and went to the porch. A letter from Ben, her first-born, and from her sister Esther—two threads connecting her to all she longed for.

She was given the chance to read a description of the house Ben was building in a suburb of Dallas—patio, sun porch, swimming pool. It was wonderful! She was so proud of him. He was a buyer for a chain of department stores and doing well, thank God. Married to a lovely girl, a baby on the way. A good head, Fanny thought. He knew the value of a dollar. He had waited to marry until he had money in the bank. "And there will be an extra bedroom, Mama," he wrote, "whenever you want to come. Marilyn will need help with the baby." There were hints that it was time for her to get out of the store and take life easy.

And she thought of what it would be like to be free, for the first time in years. She could visit Stanley, who was a computer serviceman in Cleveland or even go to live with Ben in Dallas. But Moe would never leave this Godforsaken place, though she could never understand what he found to keep him here. But when she thought of giving up the store or of moving to a strange city, even to be with the children, the prospect frightened her. She had been away from the city for so many years. The noise . . . the rush. Esther was still there in New York, married to a doctor. She had never left. Her life had been a long unbroken strand.

As she read Esther's letter, her attention kept slipping away from the latest bits of family news and complaint, and she was remembering how it had been when they both were young. It was hard on the folks, with so many kids, struggling in a new land. They had such dreams then— Poor as they were, no one was ever turned away from Sadie Kovnat's table. One big family, friends wandering in, the neighbors . . . She always liked being with Mama in the kitchen. Mama had never learned to read and write. Papa was against her going to evening classes to learn English. Fanny and the others taught her.

She remembered how she went out for her first job. The boys went on to high school, but the girls went to work. She'd been only twelve then, but she'd put her hair up in coils around her head so that she could lie about her age. "How much older Fanny looks that way," Mama had said with admiration. "She looks sixteen." She went to work sewing hats, but what an evil temper, what a wicked tongue that Russian woman had! No one could bear her. Next she worked for an Irishman in the wholesale grocery business, who'd never have hired her if he'd known first that she was Jewish. But he was very good to her. She could see him yet—red hair and blue eyes. A wonderful sense of humor.

It had been hard going with the family then, for Papa had gotten into spiritualism and horse racing, and he spent all his money on mediums and bets. The girls were just as bad. Ah, all the money they lost on dollar stocks. The dreams— But thank God, the others had married well. She could see them all so clearly. "Oh, Hattie! Esther! Mama! Papa!" The salt tears flowed as she kept looking back and looking back. "It is a terrible thing to leave your home."

But what came to him out of that night but darkness; what did it bring him to but death?

For weeks and months afterward, a payment was exacted from him in the form of tasks, duties, obligations that put him back into the framework of all he had slipped out of the way of—family and town, doctor and undertaker and rabbi.

When he came down from the Black Range, he opened the door and, to his surprise, found his sons. From that point on, he had to feel their silent reproach. While he was gone, Fanny had suffered a heart attack. An ambulance took her to the hospital, and she had asked the doctor to call her sons. For three days she hovered between life and death. On the third day she died.

People he'd had little contact with for years, but who knew and liked the boys, were suddenly there in the living room, giving their condolences. Rosie Katz, a large, handsome woman, who had been generous with her advice when Fanny started her shop, wept copiously both at the funeral and in the living room, tears streaking her rouge. And Anna Silberman, who was in her eighties but still in her store every day, took a little time off for a visit. "She was a good little business-woman," she said, nodding her head. "I have to hand it to her."

They all came, those who had known Fanny in the way of business or friendship. And as he sat there, uncomfortable in the first suit he had owned for years, and looked at them across the gulf that divided them, he was filled with sadness. They had not come for his sake, but that was all right. In a way, perhaps they did. They had brought food enough for an army, asking him and the boys again and again what they could do for them. They meant so well; on such occasions they were full of kindness. And the sadness went to his depths.

The crowd of people at the funeral unnerved him. The long hours waiting at the hospital, the presence of his sons, the shock of Fanny's death, and the sense of something permanently unresolved, left him on the verge of weeping. And yet he could not weep in public. At home afterwards, when he was alone, he took off his clothes, as slowly as he had ever done anything, hung them neatly in the closet, and lay down and sank into sleep as though he had fallen to the bottom of a pit.

The boys took charge of everything—the will, the disposition of the stock in the store, the bills, the letters. They were continually thrusting papers in front of him for his signature, asking him at first whether he wanted them to do this or that, then simply going ahead and doing he knew not what. He had no questions; whatever they did was fine with him. He embraced them when they left for Cleveland and Dallas. What would he have done without them? They knew how to manage things.

Then he was left alone, the house fearfully empty. He looked at the family pictures on the wall, on a background of flowered wallpaper Fanny had chosen. He looked at the furniture she had picked out and was reminded everywhere of what no longer existed. In a few days he went to see a realtor and put the house up for sale. He moved into Mrs. Slater's Boarding House.

It had been weeks since he had been outside the town, weeks he had lived in a fog of grief and guilt. He hardly knew what he was doing, where he was going. Always something nagged at the back of his mind that would not let go of him or give him any peace.

One afternoon late in August, he walked out to the cemetery on the hill just above the town and stood at the foot of Fanny's grave. There was no granite stone there yet, not for a year, but all around her were monuments. The community had claimed her, given her a home.

He took off his hat, the hat that seemed the color of weather, of the sun that had baked it and the rain that had drenched it, and bowed his head. She was gone, and he wondered if, in the final pressure of her hand, she had forgiven him. He couldn't blame her—all she wanted was to know where the next meal was coming from, to see that the boys had a good start in life. Who could blame her for that?

The tall brown grass was a tawny hide on the hills, and as he listened, he could hear the deep murmur of summer. His gaze wandered off to the horizon, where the blue of the distant peaks faded into the inner shell of sky streaked with pink and ivory, far beyond the reach of the eye. It was like a dream. And it seemed as though he could stand there forever listening to the crickets intoning their summer chant, singing of earth and the mountains, of all the things that would never die.

July

Something was happening to the old man, that was clear. As though someone had lifted his mind from the rest of him, as one might steal a sombrero and leave a man bareheaded in the sun. Just that morning, July had had to catch him by the sleeve to keep him from stepping into the street right in front of an oncoming car. Then the old man came round for a moment and, snatching his arm away, protested, "It's okay, it's okay—I saw him coming." Once across the street, though, he'd faded back into whatever world he'd momentarily abandoned for this one and shuffled on down the street, mumbling to himself. As he was doing now, though fortunately he was in the truck, where July could keep an eye on him. When he could take his eyes from the road that wound through the mountains, he gave the old man a sidelong glance.

He wanted the old man to shut up. He wanted to shrug him off and not have to listen anymore. July couldn't understand him, wouldn't have been able to understand him even if he had been talking Spanish, or rather the sort of do-it-yourself lingo he'd patched together from pieces of both languages. *Donde está the frying pan?* July spoke the same sort of English, so they never came up short when they tried to say what they wanted or what the situation called for, the lack in one being made up by the other. From that same spirit of negotiation or compromise July had got his name, for in Spanish it was Julio. But July was what the old man called him, till it seemed like his other name was lost with all the other things he'd left behind. And he would never know if the old man had cheated him of something or offered him what he'd never have had otherwise.

Mostly they spoke through their work, laying brick and mixing mortar and building patios and painting houses, mowing lawns and clipping grass—whatever fell to hand. They spoke through that intuitive knowledge that allowed them to go to the next stage of the work, pick up the right tool, knock off for lunch or quit for the day, without really having to speak. Their silences over the years had knitted them together more powerfully than the words passing between them—had made their true speech.

Only now it was different. The old man seemed closed off by whatever was going through his head, caught in it like a web. And his speaking was in another language altogether, mournful and sour as though he'd dug up an old anger, an ancient, rotting grief long buried. July couldn't fathom it. Even when he understood the words, he didn't know where they belonged. For he'd never thought about the old man's life, the part that ribboned back beyond their time together. Just as he seldom thought of his own, back in the village with his mother: the bewildering comings and goings of men, none of whom seemed to be his father; the fretting and gossip of the women who called themselves aunts; and the rough play of sisters, brothers, cousins. The impulse that had sent him running off to Juárez had come into his life like a surprise visit from a stranger. He couldn't explain how it had taken hold of him, just a boy, and set him there on the streets alone, without thought of where he would go, how he would eat. But perhaps the same impulse had also made him canny. He'd seen the old man—even then he had seemed old—not exactly *borracho*, but at the point where the tongue is thick and words begin to blur, and the *here* moves over to *there* and wavers with the passage. He had seen it before, when he was young enough that his eyes saw and his ears heard without a knowing. When laughter rang in his ears and made him draw back as though from a menace, and men wept without sorrow or waved their arms and roared without disturbing the flies on the wall.

He saw the old man and followed him into a café. When the old man sat at a table, he came up boldly and sat down op-

posite him, as though they had entered together. And when
he looked at the old man, whose blond hair had lightened into
white above a dry, weathered face, whose beaked nose gave
him the look of an old bird of prey, and whose eyes were a
worn brown, maybe tired of looking, he was not afraid. He did
not say then that his future was sitting across from him, but
he must have known at first glance. And when the waiter
came, he spoke up and ordered after the old man had ordered.

After he had eaten and before the waiter brought the bill, he
slipped away outdoors. But the old man hadn't sent him away,
had even asked him was he hungry, and nodded when he
asked the waiter for caldillo, which he had never eaten in his
village. He thought about it, then went back inside to the
table. The old man looked at him as though adjusting his
focus to make sure he was really there. You live around here?
he asked the boy in Spanish. The boy shook his head. Where
do you sleep? He shrugged.

Bueno, the old man said. A place to sleep and food in the
belly. But only if you work . . . *trabajar para comer*. He
watched the old man pay the bill and get up to leave, not too
steady on his feet. He followed alongside, and let the old man
put a hand on his shoulder to steady himself. On the street, if
he didn't watch out, someone could reach inside his pocket,
take his wallet. For a moment the boy's hand trembled.

Taxi? he asked the old man, and hailed one. Together they
went across the border. And together they remained.

The old man had a truck bed he'd fitted up as a sort of
shelter and a place to keep his tools. He had a hot plate and a
cot and a shelf for canned goods. He had a shotgun for hunting
and a pole for fishing. His clothes hung on hooks on the wall.
The boy slept on a mat on the floor, comfortable enough, and
watched as the old man fried eggs for their breakfast, looked
on with interest as he heated up stew in a pan for their supper.
Looked out at the unfolding landscape and the mountains
disappearing into the flatland, as they drove from El Paso to
the east.

At first, he handed the old man his tools when he needed
them, cleaned trowels and brushes, clipped grass, opened

sacks of cement. He learned to pound in a nail and handle a brush and lay brick and mix cement. The old man could do any kind of work, and he learned to do it, too. Till they worked side by side, two workers instead of one, and they ate together in the café in whatever town they had landed for the moment, and when he looked old enough, they drank two beers together in the bar afterward.

In all their time together, he saw the old man drunk only once. He'd been in a poker game, lost money—July didn't know how much. And he'd stood up, threatening, cursing, accusing somebody of marking the cards. It was only because he was drunk and July had got him back to the truck before one of the men had answered the insults with a knife that the old man had come away unharmed. In the truck he ranted for an hour: *ten fortunes won and lost. You people thinking they could run everything themselves. Rob a man of his life and all he's worked to gain.* The next day the old man remembered scarcely anything that had happened, seemed ashamed of the rest. Would never drink or allow July more than two beers. "Cards and liquor and women—that's all it takes to ruin a man. You remember that." And after that, the old man kept hold of his money—his and July's, too.

So they'd moved from town to town, wherever there was work, little jobs: putting in steps, shoring up a wall, fixing anything broken—jobs too small for most workingmen to be bothered with or to count on making a living at. All across Texas they went in the beat-up old truck, and back; then into New Mexico and as far as Arizona when the cold weather came on. A couple of times at the beginning he'd been made to go to school, but fortunately not for long. He wasn't the kind to sit at a desk and put his mind to things that had happened long before he was even born. He was happy when they moved on, and he could do as he liked. *Trabajar para comer*, as the old man had said. He'd swallowed the old man's words, had taken the old man's terms: it was all he asked.

Seven years had come and gone. He even had a little money, for although the old man took most of it for his keep, put it away in the metal box he kept with the padlock on it underneath his cot, still he gave the boy something. There were other things in the box, too. Once, as he stood behind the old man, he caught a glimpse of a snapshot of a young woman with dark skin and a long braid of hair, who sat smiling, holding a baby. In the same box was a knife rusted in a way that made it look like blood had dried on it. But the old man never spoke of these things, never took them out to show him. And July never asked him any questions. More than anything he was surprised by the thick wad of bills in the box. It was more money than he had ever seen. But now he himself had a little money and a small mustache—it was enough.

The first time it came like a bad dream, in the middl of the night. July woke up to the sound of moaning. And as he sat listening, something much darker seemed to fill the dark. *The swamp*, the old man moaned. *Dark, filthy water all covered with brush and slime and dead snags sticking out.* That was the first time. And July could see the old man hunched forward, head bent below his knees. *Terrible. Terrible.* July didn't know what he was talking about. A place he'd never seen in all their travels, filled with things always before the old man's eyes. Things that had sunk to the bottom, swelling like old wood, then floating to the surface, surrounded by swamp gas. And more nights came when the old man sat up and howled like an animal at the full moon, troubled by what cannot be seen and lies far in the dark, but troubles the blood. Now the night came into the day, and the old man stumbled around in the midst of his confusion. Sometimes he yelled out strange things connected with nothing. Threw them into the air: *No, get back—don't ever come back!* And July instinctively looked around to see if some actual thing had invaded them. But they were alone in the truck, the night lit up by a full moon, the cottonwoods thrumming with cicadas. Nothing out there. It was as though an old movie was running inside his head, full of things he couldn't stand to see, yet couldn't get rid of. And that film shut out everything of the present moment. July found himself continually shaking the old man by the arm to rouse him, for in the middle of whatever they were doing, he'd go back to watching his movie:

he'd go off to the truck to get a tool from his toolbox and forget what he'd gone for. Then July would have to go and tell him. Or pull him back from walking into things or out into the street. He had to keep his eye on the old man every minute now: he might wander to the edge of a cliff and fall into a chasm.

Now at least he was in the truck, for a moment nodding off, half asleep. It was late afternoon and hot. July was sweating as he drove. Two hours more before the mountains brought them any coolness. They would be in the Sangre de Cristos before sunset.

But right in one of those moments when there was no thought in his mind and he had let himself go with the sound of the motor, something started going wrong with the truck. First he noticed a little smoke coming from the engine, and saw that the temperature gauge was near the top of the red. He pulled over so that he could cool the engine, look into the radiator, and pour in some water from the canvas bag hooked on the side. But even as he came to a stop, more and more smoke billowed out through the hood. He got the old man out of the truck, half pulling, half coaxing him, for he didn't know where they were or what was happening. "Fire!" July shouted. "*Fuego!*" The old man responded then, in fear, as though the whole landscape were in flames.

But July had no time for him. He rushed back to the truck and tried to get the hood open, but the smoke made him cough and the metal was too hot to touch. The truck would burn up, the gasoline explode. He leapt up into the shed and brought out their food, their clothes, the tools, and the metal box and set them in the bushes. If the truck burned up, their things would be safe.

Though smoke kept pouring out, nothing happened. The road was nearly empty. He flagged down a passing car and tried to tell the driver what had happened. The fellow said he'd call a garage. But an hour later no one had come. He didn't dare try starting the truck, and he didn't want to leave the old man alone—who seemed once again to have forgotten what had threatened and now sat on a large flat rock, as much alone as if July weren't there.

They hadn't eaten since daybreak, and his stomach rumbled unpleasantly. There was food, and he had to have some. He made a little circle of rocks, gathered some brush, and lit a fire to heat up meat and beans, which they ate with tortillas and drank down with water. He was hot and dirty from the smoke. He put the water bag to his lips and drank deeply, letting the water pour down over his chest. He felt good now, full of beans. He walked around a little, his feet restless. He wanted to go somewhere, and there was nowhere to go.

The afternoon sun was a glory, the land blazing under it. Just at his shoulder a mountain peak rose up with a great fleecy cloud just above it, gray at the center. The shadow made hollows in the hills, while the grasses and joshua trees took the light. It seemed to July that the sky had never reached so far, nor the land, in its expansiveness. Miles it traveled to the horizon. He could see so far. And when he turned and let his eyes lift to the crest of the peak, the mountain seemed to enter him, the cloud pouring down over him, the bluff forming inside him. For the first time he was struck by the land, as something to possess and wound him, as something to wonder at and feel its power. He stood, listening to the fullness of summer humming in the air around him. It had rained almost every day that spring, and the mountains were covered with grass. And there he was standing out in the sun, no trowel or hammer in his hand, looking at the little yellow and white flowers. He breathed deeply, felt something in him rising to the surface, strong and full. He looked out as if it had suddenly been given for him to rule over this empire of summer, to take the land in his embrace. And he wanted something with a desire that drove into him like a thorn and teased him beyond words to where he felt only rage and frustration.

Innocente! Innocente! Tu eres mi hijo. The old man was looking at him as though he wanted to convince him of something that would put him off, or else put down some fear inside himself. His son? It was a lie—the old man speaking into the air again things that had no meaning. Innocent—and what did he mean? His son. What were these words? Something the old man had made up to throw around him like a rope, to make some claim upon him he didn't understand and which would bind and imprison him?

Y tu eres un loco, the boy thought with sudden knowledge. Crazy. That was what had happened—the old man was out of his head.

For a long time the boy sat, blowing through a blade of grass between his thumbs, then biting the sweetness from the long stems of the wild grasses. The afternoon was waning, the sky paling above the mountains, opposite which the sun would soon be gone. There were no clouds now, just a fading blue above a pale orange. The truck was quiet now, the fire having burned itself out.

But they must find a place for the night. It would be dark soon, and the night would be cold once the sun moved behind the hills. First the valleys would fill with shadow and the pleasant heat would be pulled away. Even their jackets would not keep them warm. He dare not leave the old man alone; he could wander into the middle of the road and be killed. They would have to do what he had been putting off doing—walk he didn't know how far to the nearest house or pay phone or town. Fortunately, the old man was still strong; he didn't have to carry him along. He went to the bushes where he had hid their things and picked up the money box. "*Vente*," he said to the old man. "We have to find somebody. "*Andale pues*."

They had to walk for a long time. Till the sun had set and it grew dark. They had to stop to rest twice before they came to the red neon lights of the sign that sat in the pines with no promise of a town beyond it: Solano Bar—Café. Two cars and a motorcycle were parked in front, where more neon advertised Miller's High Life. They went inside and sat down at one of the booths.

The bar girl passed July, gave a glance in his direction, and smiled. "Get you in a minutes, sweetie," she said.

July smiled at her.

"What can I get you?" she said when she came back. Her hair was a bunch of curls that had escaped over her forehead as though they'd grown through a fence, and she had a little full mouth and a cleft chin. The way she tilted her head and looked at July made him grin at her.

"Hey, you got a nice smile," she said.

He ducked his head, then looked at her. She was grinning at him.

"Beer," he said. "*Quieres cerveza?*" he asked the old man.

"Whiskey. I want whiskey."

"Beer is better," July said. What had set him off? He wasn't used to whiskey. And if the old man got drunk, he would have to carry him. Even if he found a taxi or somebody gave them a ride, it would be just one more trouble.

"Shot of whiskey," the old man said, bringing his fist down on the table.

"What's with him?" the girl wanted to know.

July shrugged. Suddenly he wished he were rid of the old man. "Okay," he said, "Whiskey and beer. A Miller's."

The old man downed the shot as soon as the girl set it in front of him. "Hit me again, lady," he demanded. "You sweet little thing."

July looked at the girl. She did not like the old man, he could tell. She did not want him calling her "sweet little thing." If he did again, July would tell him to stop.

July shrugged. He did not want trouble. They would take a taxi. The old man would be drunk. He would take the keys out of his pocket and open up the box and take money for a room in a hotel. The thought gave him a sudden thrill. He was in charge; he had been put in charge without knowing it. Now he knew. And he would take charge of the box.

"Okay," he said to the girl. "And another one for me, too." Thirstily, he drank off his beer. It pleased him to watch her walk away, and it would be good when she came back. He liked her smile. He wanted to make her laugh. It would feel good to make her laugh.

The old man had begun to mutter to himself, and it came out with an ugly sound, though July couldn't make out the words. When he drank down his whiskey, he demanded a bottle.

"Look, man . . ." July protested, as though reason might lie in the English language.

"I'm getting my bottle." He rose up from the table and started forward, July catching him by the arm.

"I've throttled better men than you," the old man snarled, shaking him off, surprisingly strong. "And I don't mind doing it now."

July glanced over to where the girl was talking in an anxious way to the bartender.

"You want to get us thrown out?" July grabbed him again. "*Sientate!*" he shouted. He was angry now; he'd have liked to hit the old man across the face. He could imagine the blow. He felt something harden in his own face as he spoke. He had not felt his face stiffen like that before, and it surprised him.

The bartender was coming over. "What's going on?" he demanded. "You make trouble and you get thrown out. Understand?" Then he said to July, "What's the matter with the guy, anyway?"

July tapped a finger against the side of his head. "He won't do nothing—he has forgotten."

He was shoving the old man back into the booth, making him sit down. He couldn't tell anymore whether the old man was forgetting or remembering or whether it was all things that had never happened, like lies in his head—if that is what it was to be crazy. And now the voice returned, as of an old grief. The old man moaned, then wailed in a strange, almost feminine voice: "*Muerto. Por qué? Por qué?*"

Someone had died. Or had the old man killed someone? His imagination flew to the rusty knife in the box. Perhaps the old man had killed many men, all unknown and gone, and the knife had grown rusty over the years. All the blood.

The old man was shaking his head as if he wanted to shake loose what was inside it. But July had hold of his arm, held him hard and made him sit down. "He will do nothing," July said. He was in charge, and the old man would obey him.

The girl came over with his beer and another whiskey. "This is for the old guy," she said. "But no more."

"But how about me?" he said, grinning at her again. "Can I make you run back and bring me beer to fill my thirst?"

"Sure," she said.

"And how about if I buy a drink for you?" he said. "Will you sit down?" He patted the bench.

"Why not?" she said. "There's nobody around. This dump is about as dead as yesterday's beer."

He pulled some money out of his pocket. "Here," he said "Whatever you like."

In a moment she brought back a drink, something green the light shone through, and sat down next to him. He was intrigued.

"Well," she said, "here's to us," and they clinked glasses. "You're a good-looking guy, you know that?"

He ducked his head again and then grinned at her.

"I mean it. What're you doing with that old fart-face?"

He'd nearly forgotten the old man, who'd grown quiet, who might as well have gone off and left him. He'd drunk off half the whiskey in the glass, which he held in his hand now as if he had forgotten what to do with it.

"He's crazy," July said, in a low voice.

She giggled and put a hand over her mouth, as though she'd gotten a sudden inspiration. "Hey, old garbage," she taunted the old man, "going to fill your brain with whiskey? What'll you do then?"

"You get out," the old man said suddenly, "or I'll put holes to bleed you into the dust."

She laughed. "You can't hurt a fly," the girl said. "You try."

"No two-timing bitch," he said, nearly pushing the table over on them, "is going to make a monkey out of me. You just try cheating around. You just try it."

July knew he wasn't even talking to them. And the girl seemed to know, too, to enjoy being part of a drama she had no understanding of.

"You tell it to me, honey," she said, leaning forward, wiggling her shoulders. "See what I got? Wouldn't you like to have some?"

"I'll kill him, too," the old man said, rising up.

"You do that, honey," she said and grinned at July. He took

her hand. He wanted her to be quiet and not set the old man off. And yet he wanted her to go on, to see what would happen if she continued to goad him. He felt strange. He wanted to laugh at the old man, and yet a certain fear came into him. He reached out and grabbed the old man by the arm.

"He's not here," he said, hoping he could put the old man off. "He's gone."

"Where is he?" he bellowed. "Tell me where the bastard's hiding."

The girl had lost interest. Her attention had found a new object. "What's in the box?" she wanted to know.

"Money," he said, "and some other things."

"Money?" she said. "Money's to spend."

It occurred to him with the force of a new idea.

"Where is he?" the old man continued to holler, rising again. "I'll get him."

July felt as though he were being pulled in three directions. He was trying to quiet the old man, but he wanted to listen to the girl. But most of all, he wanted to think about what was inside the box.

"Go get him," the girl taunted him. "Out in back. Go get him."

The old man pulled himself out of July's grasp, and July could not keep him back. He lurched in the direction of the door. "Hey, man," July called, getting up to follow him.

"Stay here," the girl said to him. "Stay with me. Much better without him."

He stood uncertainly. The old man had found the outside door at the back and was fumbling with the knob. And he was the other, standing there, caught, with one foot about to step into the next moment, as into a strange place, and discover what he had never known before. Yet he wanted something to happen. He wanted a change. He did not care what the old man had done or if he had done anything. He wanted now to put him out of his mind and forget about him, to be rid of him. He wanted to put his arm around the girl next to him and touch her breast. He wanted to buy her another drink and hear her laugh. And to come the next night and drink some more and laugh and buy drinks for all the men. The girl was squeezing his hand. The old man had opened the door now and staggered outside, and if he didn't go out after him something would happen. The old man would fall down in the dark and never get up again. But then, if he went now and brought him in, he would have to carry him on his back, maybe till he was worn out.

Something else inside was urging him on, something that was the strength in his arm and the energy in his body. Something that he wanted to grab and devour and then toss away the rind. Now. The old man had had his time. He didn't want to stay there in the dark and he didn't want to carry the old man on his back. He wanted to be off and never look behind him. He had a life. Right now.

Lucinda

The night before, Alex had come, arriving sometime after midnight. Pilar sat up in bed, first hearing the car door slam, then the sound of the key in the lock. She slipped out of bed without turning on the light, hoping not to wake Lucinda, who lay in a warm curl beside her, her small chest rising and falling with her breath. When Alex was gone, Lucinda slept in his place.

"You are here," she said, going into the living room, blinking against the light. He had thrown his windbreaker across the chair and was sitting on the couch, taking off his tennis shoes, grunting and groaning like an old man.

"I'm beat. All the fucking trucks on the highway. Crowd a man. Have to take up the whole goddam road. Oh, God, I am fucking tired."

"Do you want me to rub your back?" she asked.

He worked his shoulders around—heavy, muscled shoulders. "Thanks," he said. "But I'm too goddam tired to stay up for it. Just got to get me some shut-eye." He heaved himself off the couch and into the bedroom, Lucinda's room.

Pilar stood in the doorway, watching him take off his shirt and undo his belt. He looked fat and tan, as though he'd soaked up all the sun he could find out there on the Coast, put some of it on his shoulders and the rest on his belly. He was a burly man, thick, carrying a load at the middle. Too much food, too much beer, Pilar thought as she gazed at him. Now he was there—back. She did not know exactly where he'd been and what he'd done—that is, what he had brought back with him, what she was supposed to do with it.

"You just gonna stand there?" Alex wanted to know. "Look, kid, you ain't getting nothing out of me tonight. Right now, I'm no more good than a spavined horse." He flopped heavily onto the bed, made it groan.

She turned out the light and went back to Lucinda. When she slipped under the covers, Lucinda turned over, murmured something in her sleep and nuzzled against her. Pilar touched her on the shoulder, not enough to wake her, and lay in the dark for a moment, taking in the warm, sweet scent of her childhood.

Alex was home—for how long this time? It was his way, to come in like a change of weather, like a cloud of dust on the desert, or a cloudburst that sends the rivers roaring through the arroyos. Without warning. And when he came, it was always different, and when he left something changed with him. She lay in the dark wondering why this was, and how it would be now with his coming.

It did not always happen, it was true. His dealings took him away for days or weeks at a time. And things went on the same. She was used to his comings and goings, to the many conversations on the telephone, often in Spanish, of which he knew enough to take care of things. *"Tiene usted el dinero!"* she would hear him ask, with an intensity she had come to recognize. And the amount of pesos he mentioned was more than she had ever seen. So much money. She did not know all the numbers even to count it. What would anyone do with so much money?

She could not tell how it would be this time. A month he had been away, in Los Angeles. Making deals. Buying, selling—she did not know what. She never asked him, he never told her. Sometimes he came back, singing at the top of his lungs, smirking like a well-fed tomcat. Then he'd pick her up and swing her around, and say, "Well, my chiquita, we'll do the town up brown. Do some of them nightclubs over in Juárez." But he'd never taken her back over there. She was just as glad.

Other times he complained about the fleabag hotels he'd put up in or the time he had spent waiting for José or Gary or

Fulgencio or some other stranger to turn up, but these were the only clues she had as to where he'd been or how he'd spent his time. She did not want to know.

Once, not long after he'd brought her across the border, she'd been frightened nearly out of her head. When she was alone, she kept the door locked, as Alex had told her to do. And she seldom went out by herself. But this time somebody kept banging on the door till she had to open it. Maybe it was La Señora who'd rented them the room. But no, a policeman stood in front of her in the doorway, demanding to know where Alex was. She could not tell him, nor could she understand what he was saying, though he tried a few words of Spanish, and she tried to use the English words Alex had taught her.

She was afraid the man had come to take her back to Juárez. But she had been wrong. He ended up by writing on a piece of paper, *The feds are wise,* and disappeared. So did Alex for nearly a month—and in that way she came to understand what the words meant. That was the first change, her worrying that he was gone and would never come back. And what would she do then, when her money ran out? The rent was paid, but there was only a little left for food. Then one day he was back. They moved out of the little room in the barrio into another part of the city. After that, she never asked him any questions. There was money, she did not care how he got it. She had a good place to live, with electricity and running water, and food on the table, and clothes to wear. But that had begun the changes. They had moved many times now, from one apartment to another. This was the best—clean, and the toilet worked, and there was a yard for Lucinda to play in. If she needed something, Pilar asked Alex for it. At first, she asked timidly, afraid he would be angry. But he would reach in his pocket and pull out a five-dollar bill, or even a ten and give it to her, as if he didn't care. Sometimes he gave without her asking. But unless it was to buy some present for Lucinda, she had little to ask for.

Now, for the first time, in this place she had a friend, Sarah—Sally, as she liked to be called, and it was good to have a friend. They were all Americans in these apartments, and Pilar was shy about speaking to them—her English was not so good, although she had learned a lot by listening to the television, repeating what it said. But Sally did not seem to mind her having to pause sometimes to reach for a word. She was alone as well, had just gotten a divorce from her husband—"the no-good son-of-a-bitch. He screwed me over plenty, let me tell you." She talked a lot about him. She was teaching Pilar some new words.

That morning Pilar got up early and went into the kitchen to see what she might do to make a surprise for Lucinda. It was a game they had. Sometimes she peeled an orange or a banana and made a little figure out of the peelings. Or she arranged slices of fruit in a design on Lucinda's plate. After she had made her surprise, she would go to wake Lucinda. The child would be lying there, breathing so softly, the flush of sleep on her cheeks, her eyes closed with the long fine fringe of her lashes, her lips slightly parted. Asleep, she was like a creature from another world. Pilar found it hard to believe this was her own child. She would wake her, and watch her yawn and stretch as she came into the morning from wherever she had been. For a moment the sleep would stay with her. Then her eyes grew bright as she remembered. "What is my surprise?" she demanded, and without waiting a moment longer, she ran into the kitchen to see.

"A bird, you made a bird—*qué bueno!*"

Today when Pilar went to wake her, she put a finger over her lips. Lucinda caught on immediately:

"*Papá está aquí?*" she asked in a whisper.

"*Sí,*" she said, whispering too. "*Muy cansado.*"

"I will be very quiet," Lucinda said, her eyes lighting up. Whispering was a game, too. She would play the Whisper Game. And the Tiptoe Game, and the Moving-Very-Quietly Game. Pilar watched her elaborate pantomime, and her expression, all very exaggerated. Such a clever little rascal she was—her little parakeet, her mouse, her bee.

"Come into the kitchen, *mija,*" Pilar told her.

"Do you have a surprise for me?" Lucinda wanted to know.

"I have a surprise," she said. "A small surprise. And maybe there will be another," she said. "A special surprise."

"Something to eat?" Lucinda wanted to know.

"No, something else."

"When?"

"Later." Sally brought it over to Pilar last night when Lucinda was asleep. Sally had brought other things, candy and books with pictures in them, that Pilar and Lucinda had sat and looked at together. "I love that little kid," Sally said, and that made Pilar feel very proud of her. She wanted to give Lucinda her surprise right then, but Alex would be waking soon, and it would not be the right moment. It was different now that he was home. She had been alone with the child for so long, she hardly knew how to act with him there. They had their special ways. She would save her surprise until the right moment. For now, she had an orange on which she had made a face, with raisins for eyes and a smile cut out of the skin. She'd made a little paper cone hat to put on its head and set it up on a glass. Lucinda didn't want to eat the orange man—she named him Pepe.

As soon as Lucinda finished breakfast, Pilar let her go outside to play on the swings and slides at the center of the apartment complex. Usually, when they came home from the grocery store, she stayed outside with Lucinda and watched her play in the sandbox or pushed her in one of the swings. But when Alex was there, her whole routine changed. Otherwise, she would have gone first to the store with Lucinda. Lucinda loved to shop in the grocery. They went every day. Lucinda would pick out the vegetables and fruit and put them into a bag. She took boxes of cereals from the shelves, and picked out the kind of soap they would use, sniffing different ones till she found a scent she liked. It always took a very long time for them to do their shopping, most of the morning, in fact. And then the swings and slides. Sometimes now, though, Pilar spent time with Sally.

Just as Pilar finished making the coffee, Alex came into the kitchen, dressed in a faded checked shirt that he liked to wear and a clean pair of blue jeans. He still hadn't shaved, but he was feeling good, she could tell, punching his fist into his hand, as though he had new energy he needed to get rid of.

"Did you sleep well?" she asked him.

"Like a goddam brick," he said. "Boy, was I beat. Christ A-mighty. Today I'm just going to re-lax, have me a few beers and lie around. I don't wanna see no inside of a car."

She gave him a cup of coffee—she'd made a big pot, because he would drink many cups of coffee. She poured one for herself, half coffee, half milk, and sat down with him.

"You know," Alex said, "that Los Angeles is quite a place. Lots going on out there."

She'd heard him say so before. And there was a program she watched on TV that had interested her because it was set in Los Angeles. She liked the palm trees and the ocean. Once she had even felt a desire to go. "All the movie stars live there," she said.

"That ain't the half of it," he said. "Everytime I go out there, I think, what am I doing in a dinky place like this? Out there, they've got some style."

She wasn't quite sure what he meant, but she wondered if this was to be a new change. Did he want to move again? After they had come to this apartment with a place for Lucinda to play and even a friend for her to talk to? She could not imagine going to another place.

"I like it here," she said, trying only to sound pleased with the apartment. But she felt a sudden panic. If Alex were to take her somewhere else, she would have to find her way again—learn new streets, find out where the grocery was. Maybe they would not have a playground. It was such a big city—so many cars.

"Yeah," he said, "it's okay. If you got to have a place to come back to when you need it." He seemed almost to be talking to himself. "But one of these days I'd like to live it up a bit. That's what it's all about."

She said nothing. She did not want to go against him. Now she could think only of Lucinda. In the beginning, it did not matter to her where they lived. First the little room with a hot plate and a television and no backyard. Then after moving quite suddenly, half a duplex on a dusty street with weeds and cans in the backyard, and many stray cats in the sheds around—lean and hungry and fierce in the eye. They moved from there, too, because Alex said too many wise guys were trying to nose into his business. They had stayed in another set of rooms for a few months, then moved again to this place.

At first she was alone in the room all day, watching the television. When Alex came home, she sat on his lap on the sofa, and they watched together. And he taught her to heat up food on the hot plate and how to say words in English.

Then an extraordinary thing happened to her. The change had come upon her more powerfully than any change in the weather. She had not thought about it until it happened. In the beginning, she did not even know what it was, her breasts growing, her waist thickening. Then her ripening belly, her shape enlarging like that of women she had seen on the street. It had been an astonishment to her to find herself like one of them, with a baby inside her, feeling its kicking there in the dark when she was lying alone, awake while Alex lay asleep beside her, or while he was gone. It was like a secret growing in the dark, a surprise that would come when it was ready. And she wanted to laugh because a surprise was coming to her.

How she had wept and sobbed during the labor. It had frightened her very much when the pains began and Alex wasn't there. He said he would be home, and finally he came and took her to the hospital. She had never been in a hospital before, had never felt such pains tearing her apart, not even when she was hungry. But afterward there was the baby. Her child: with golden skin, lighter than hers, but with her own dark lustrous hair. Alex had been the one to name the baby: Lucinda. At first the name sounded a little strange in her ear, as though it were trying to be Spanish. But it was made in America. She liked the sound of it, its music. She made up little pet names to call her—*Lita* and *Lulinda* and *Lucita*. And she carried the baby around everywhere and sang to her and talked to her and watched her while she slept.

She had no thought for anything else while the baby nursed at her breast, filling up with milk till she got drowsy and fell asleep. Or when she fed her with a spoon or held her or shook a rattle until she grabbed it. Alex left her alone with the child. He was gone more and more all the time. And Pilar was glad to be alone with Lucinda. If he was at home, he sometimes looked at Lucinda, as if he were wondering where she came from, as if she had not been made in America but in a strange place and not by him. She did not look like him at all. Sometimes he picked her up and swung her around by her arms or held her upside down. And Pilar was filled with terror that he would hurt her. But Lucinda squealed with delight. Sometimes now she ate with them. But usually it was late when they had their meal, too late for her, with her active body and her young appetite, to wait for them. Pilar used to feed Lucinda in the kitchen and put her in the playpen. Now Lucinda could go out to play with her friends. Lucinda was five.

After he had his breakfast, Alex sat on the couch and watched the game shows on television, then flipped through a magazine. Around noon, he got up, said, "I'm going out to get me some beer and talk to some guys. Then I'll come home and watch the ball game."

After she had done the dishes, she found Lucinda and they went to the grocery store. The car was still gone when they came back, so they went over for a little while to visit Sally.

"See your man's home," Sally said.

"He came in the middle of the night."

"Well, I'm glad to get rid of mine—lying and cheating like the bastard he was. I tell you, I don't know what it is with men— Only now I got to get me a new one. Somebody who'll take care of me and treat me right."

"I hope you find somebody," Pilar told her. "It is hard to be alone."

"You're lucky, you know. You got one that's not underfoot overmuch, that's the main thing—and you got that sweet little kid. That Lucinda," she said. "You want a cookie, honey?"

Pilar smiled, proud of her child.

"Guess she'll be starting school one of these days," Sally said.

"She is too young," Pilar said. She did not want to think about it—Lucinda going away from her. School seemed as far away as Los Angeles. Lucinda would go to school and learn how to read, and soon she would know more than her mother. Pilar had gone as far as the second grade, but she had forgotten most of what she had learned. She could read Spanish words, some of them. Lucinda already knew more English than she did, for the children she played with did not know Spanish.

"I better go now," she said, seeing Alex drive up.

Sally came out of her apartment with her, and when Alex got out of the car, Pilar said, "This is Sally."

"Glad to meetcha," Alex said and gave her his hand, a big hand. "Just got back from L.A."

"You have a good time?" Sally said.

"You bet," he said. "Just got me some beer there in the car," he said. "Why don'cha come over later on and have one?"

"Sure," she said, looking at Pilar. "Sure thing."

When she and Alex went back to the apartment, Pilar told him how Sally had moved in while he was gone and how kind she was to Lucinda. It was the first time she had talked to him about someone he did not know. This time he did not seem to mind. Once a boy on the street had come up to her and asked her if she lived in the neighborhood. When she came home, Alex told her not to speak to strangers.

Sally came over with a bowl of popcorn she had made, and Pilar set out some tortillas and chili sauce to eat while they drank the beer. For a while they all watched the ball game, then afterward a comedy. Pilar didn't understand some of the jokes, but it didn't matter. Afterward, Sally and Alex started talking about L.A. Sally had lived there for a year way back when, and together they talked about the places they knew, the best bars to hang out in, and how bad the smog was.

"Used to work in a music store out there on the Sunset Strip," Sally said. "Nice place. That's where I met my ex, damn his hide. He was trying to be a country singer, and he used to buy all the albums. Me, I was just trying to get by."

"Ain't we all?" Alex said. "Time you get done working to get from one day to the other, you're about all wore out."

"You can say that again," Sally said.

Alex liked Sally, Pilar could tell. Sally laughed a lot, and it was nice when she laughed. She was not young, and her face had gone hard in a way, especially when she talked about what her man had done. But now she was enjoying herself. And pretty soon, she and Alex were joking with each other as if they'd known each other forever, and Alex was telling her things he'd done in L.A. How he had a friend who had a Harley-Davidson, which was the only kind of motorcycle to have—none of your crummy Jap machines—and how he used to go out and really ride the thing, even on the freeways. He was fixing to buy one. "How'd you like to go out for a little spin?" he said to Pilar, pulling a bit of her hair. "Bet that would give you a thrill." Then they drank some more beer and laughed some more. Pilar laughed with them, for the air was light around them. He and Sally could speak very well to one another, Pilar thought. She admired how they spoke English. Lucinda was lying on the floor watching television, not paying any attention to them.

"By the way," Sally said, "how did Lucinda like the coloring book?"

Flustered, Pilar said, "Oh, I forgot. I haven't given it to her yet."

"Oh, well," Sally said, "It don't make no never-mind." And she took another drink of her beer.

"It was a nice surprise," Pilar said. She did not know how to explain.

"Well, give it to her now," Alex said. "No law against it, you know."

She went to get it. "Here," she said, giving it to Lucinda. "It is a surprise from Sally."

Lucinda looked at the box of colored crayons and the book.

"You can color any of the pictures, honey," Sally said.

Gravely, Lucinda opened the box and looked at the colors, then at Pilar. *"Me gusta mucho,"* she said excitedly, and for a long time she sat looking at the pictures in the coloring book and putting the crayons in different order in the box, taking them out again, laying them on the floor and putting them back. She asked Sally to tell her how to put them back the way they had come, then she closed the box. Pilar could tell she was sleepy and led her off to bed, putting the crayons and the coloring book on the shelf till morning.

Pilar was happy. She didn't listen anymore to what Alex was saying, she just ate popcorn and drank beer till Sally said she had to get to bed early—next morning she had to go out to look for a job.

"Hey, listen," Alex said, "the night's young. No need to rush off. Hey, why don't we go out on the town and do it up brown? Take in some of those nightclubs over the line."

Sally hesitated. "Well, I really . . ." she said.

"Come on," Alex insisted. "The three of us. Have some fun."

"But Lucinda," Pilar said.

"She's asleep," Alex said. "We'll lock the door. She'll be okay. Nothing's gonna get her."

But Pilar did not want to leave her. Things could happen. But even if they didn't . . . She might wake up and if no one was there, she'd be frightened.

"You go," she said. "I will stay here and you go—you and Sally."

"Hey, I don't like to do that," Sally said.

"It's okay," Pilar insisted. "You go, and the next time I'll go."

"Suits me," Alex said.

That night Pilar slept badly. In her dreams she was traveling somewhere, but she did not know where she was going. She was alone. When she woke up, she wasn't sure at first where she was. She found Alex heavily asleep on the couch, still in his clothes, his arm flopping over the edge to the floor.

Lucinda was still asleep. Pilar opened the door softly and went outside. A bank of cloud extended over part of the city, but beyond it the sky was a rich blue, so filled with light that everything stood out against it with a sharpness that made it seem caught there forever in utmost clarity. The dark blue mountain closest and the pink mountain farther away, so clear, so bright it was like looking at a picture. For a long time she did not move.

She thought of the colors of Lucinda's crayons, and she remembered her time at school. The teacher had given her a piece of paper and a little box of crayons, but she could not think of anything to draw. She had made a yellow mark on the paper, then a red one. Then a little box out of the red, and a little circle out of the yellow. But some of the children had made flowers and cats and people. That was long ago, long before her mother had sent her out of the house, when the neighbor had told her mother that Pilar was no longer a virgin. For a time she had slept under bridges and in abandoned cars, begging for coins from the tourists and rummaging through the refuse barrels behind the restaurants. Till some other girls told her about the hotel, where she could come and they would give her food and a place to stay, and even pay her money. And there Alex had found her. She was fourteen then.

When she went back inside, Alex was already up and dressed. He didn't want any breakfast—he was going out for awhile, didn't know when he'd be back. She wondered if he had asked Sally to go with him. Once she had seen him put his arm around a woman that he was talking to in the street, and they had gone off together. Perhaps he would go off with Sally—even as far as Los Angeles. She did not know if that was the change he had brought this time.

She went into the kitchen to make breakfast for Lucinda. Soon she would wake her. This morning she had fresh cherries to give her, and after she ate, she would give her the coloring book with the pictures already drawn. And together they would open the box of crayons and make blue dogs and red horses and green houses, with a blue sky and a yellow sun shining over all.

Of Memory and Desire

The boy is become a legend now in these parts, in the way of things that lie partly buried in the past, partly out of it, like the ruins of the Indians who once lived here, or like the *pichu cuate*, the snake said to live in this region, so deadly that one bite proves fatal. Now and then, you come upon an old man or an ancient woman who claims to have seen the square-headed snake and who, with a look and a knowing smile at those who would doubt or deny, repeats, *"Pero yo lo he visto."* It lives deep under the rocks, eluding all efforts at capture. They say its secret lies in its cleverness in lying very still, waiting, blending in with the rocks. Then, whsst, when you come upon it, it disappears, leaving you only an impression of color and movement. As if to say, *I live . . . make no mistake about that. But you won't catch me—no, only a glimpse is all you get.* You won't find the snake in a bottle being preserved in alcohol in some museum of natural history. Even so, there are those who say it is a real living creature and believe that as strongly as they believe anything. And when you hear them, hear the thrill of insistence in their voices, you would believe, too, if it meant denying the world before your eyes.

In that way, there are those who claim that the boy still lives here in the valley, and who have heard him on certain nights of the full moon, when the sky is pale like the inside of a shell and the coyotes howl. Then, they say, he comes out to play his flute by the river. The way Goat Man taught him, long before that one night. But who speaks of that?

He was real enough once. Folks in the town remember him, though no one knew where he came from, who were his kin.

They remember a skinny young kid with large eyes, suspicious and uncertain, in the same face with a full soft mouth, red lips tender as a girl's. Goat Man wasn't any kin, and no one could say how they came together. They knew only that he had lived with him as long as they could remember. Maybe it happened like this: the boy had been part of a family that had come over the border illegally and were trying to find work. Maybe they put up one of those adobe huts that was immediately crowded with too many kids. And it was hard to keep them all fed. So that when he was old enough, he went off into the world to make it on his own. He was small for his age, and though his shoulder blades stood out from his back like two wings, there were muscles in his arms. One way or another, he found his way to the valley, to the river. Not much there: a few houses, a couple of ranches. Though the river ran through the valley, the land was poor and rocky and not much would grow there. Apple trees: they like the rocks. And grass enough for a few head of cattle. There he wandered along the river, maybe looking for work picking apples in one of the orchards. And there he had found Goat Man, who could use him, particularly in the upper branches of his trees. The boy was light and nimble. And together they picked apples and put them in baskets and ate their supper together in Goat Man's adobe hut. The boy stayed after that. He never went to school. Said he was sixteen, and they left him alone, for he had a look in his eyes that wasn't to be argued with and he'd have been trouble in the classroom. Sometimes he stood around with the other kids, there on the edge of the circle listening to their talk. They teased him some, "What are you doing with that old man? He smells like a goat and lives like a goat." He didn't take the trouble to answer back. And folks didn't try to get anything out of him. They had their own business, and he wasn't doing any harm. They got used to seeing him: small for his age, and skinny, looking more Indian than Mexican. And never any older any time you saw him. Seemed like he'd look that way the rest of his life.

They got used to him the way they had got used to Goat

Man. Somebody's around long enough, they seem part of the landscape, part of the air you breathe. You'd see the two of them in the town maybe three or four times a year, when he and Goat Man climbed into the ancient red truck with the dust-caked sides and rattled down through the valley and up into the mountains. There they bought supplies: sacks of flour and sugar and coffee and beans and rice, feed for the goats, odds and ends. And in the late summer, they sold their apples. Then they'd go back to the river, to their place. Not much of a spread. An old adobe where they lived, some pens and sheds for the goats.

Goat Man had a row of beehives as well as his goats and his apple trees. And a little stand by the road, where he sold the apples and honey and goat cheese, along with the applewood flutes he carved himself. And if you felt like staying around long enough he'd teach you to play a tune, which was maybe the only tune he knew. Nobody did, though, except the boy, and when he was done with his chores, he'd sit by the river and blow a few notes on the flute. You'd be walking down the road or fishing by the river and you'd hear a melody that rose above the breeze. At first you'd think it was a whisper of air, but then the sound would take it in, play beyond it, becoming a melody. You'd catch the melody being given back to the air and notice then that the sun was an intense band of light along the ridge of the mountains with blue above. The day had been caught there. And you'd pause and hold your breath and listen, the way you do when a bird has landed in the tree just in front of you and you want to hold it there a moment and watch it, before it flies away. And then the melody would fall back into silence the way it came, without a beginning or an ending. As though you'd just caught a snatch, happened on it. Gone before you realized. And it wasn't anything you'd hear again. Maybe he made it up as he went along, the way the day makes up clouds and shadows and streaks of light. Anyway, you got used to the boy being there like that, the way you get used to the weather.

As for Goat Man, folks had been used to him for a long time. Nobody knew how old he was. He was a dark man of middle height, with a big frame and broad shoulders, a strong man, for though he was getting on, he could still hoist up a hundred-pound sack of flour and carry it to his truck. Some folks thought he was Mexican, said they heard him speaking Spanish, but Loman Cate, who tended bar at San Juan, said he was from Europe, along the Mediterranean somewhere, maybe Greek or Sicilian, and had come there right after the war. He'd had some kind of injury or accident that had scarred his face and drawn down part of his lip. He wore a beard to cover his face, and his speech was hard to catch. The limp in his walk, the bartender said, was from pieces of shrapnel in his leg.

But other folks said that Goat Man was the boy's grandfather, and that they were both illegal aliens, the old man having come here many years before. But that was likely one of those rumors that get started up, since there are lots of illegal aliens all around these parts. Nobody took the trouble to inquire. You couldn't track them all down. For they figured that with every wetback you sent across the border, there were likely to be two to take his place. And Goat Man had been there since most people could remember. When you're in a place long enough, you begin, in an odd way, to belong to it. They talked about him because he was a local curiosity, and, besides the usual, there wasn't a whole lot to talk about: who was the father of Alva Loraine's baby and whether Loman Cate was going to survive his mother-in-law's visit; whose bank account was good and whose marriage was bad— that kind of thing. When it wears thin, you have to wait for a new supply. But they could always talk about Goat Man, because they knew so little about him. Maybe he encouraged the power of invention, seeing that no one cold prove any particular rumor was true or false.

Things change very slowly around here. Though there'd always been ranches down in this part of the valley, and apple orchards, still only a few people lived there, a few more coming every year, it was true. Some tried it for a while and left. You'd see an abandoned adobe house with the roof caving in, where some family had tried to make a go of it and given up.

The Mexicans were here first, then the Anglos started coming in. It's far from any town, and isolated. In the winter the snow comes to bury the land, leaving people stranded till the snow-plows come through. Sometimes it's impossible to get the kids to school: the buses can't make it on the road. And it's even hard to get out to the store. Or to the bar on Saturday nights, which is still the one entertainment in the valley.

Anyway, no one thought much about Goat Man and the boy till Chico Benevidez got his job in the county tax assessor's office. Chico had grown up in town in a one-room adobe hut with a dirt floor, one of six brothers and sisters and no father he could identify. When he was a boy, the newest baby had died from malnutrition, and the lady from the welfare claimed that it was his mother's fault. There was an article about it in the newspaper, and when Chico went to school he felt shame. He had gone out one evening and slashed some tires. If the cops had caught him, he would have been sent off to the state boys' school, but he didn't care. He got into enough trouble, though, playing truant. He wanted them to kick him out of school; he'd go down to Dona Ana County and pick cotton. Then he tried it out one summer. His hands got blistered, and every muscle in his back ached. He decided he didn't want to do that for the rest of his life.

What would he do, then? Already he had a burning desire and a terrible energy. If he had his dreams, they were no more powerful than his hatreds, his sense of the unfairness of things. Yet he could see himself in some other place, rich, with men working for him. In spite of everything, there must be a way. He could look around and see that people had lifted themselves up, gotten jobs, made money. True, there were families that never made it up out of the mud, never had a decent shirt on their backs. But he would do it. You had to keep your eyes open, bide your time, and grab your chance when it came along. First, he had to get out of the crummy town where everybody knew him—get as far away as possible.

If he could only join the army . . . The posters he saw in front of the post office—*Join the Army. See the world*—were probably all lies. But it was his only chance. He talked to the recruiter, who told him he'd have to graduate from high school, take tests, pass a physical. From then on he worked in school, did his homework, did calisthenics in the gym. And received a grudging recognition from his teachers, who had little help in distinguishing the gleam of intelligence from the gleam of hostility. In the army he became a machinist. And when he came out, he worked for a factory in El Paso and saved his money. Once he had a stake, he bought land in the valley. Poor land, it was true, but perhaps a stake on better land in the future. He did well with his cattle. He bought more land and more calves.

Then he got lucky. A friend of his made it in politics, and Chico got some influence in the county. Pretty soon his wife was running the little post office in the valley, and he was working in the courthouse, in the tax assessor's office. He'd come a long way in the world.

Folks had become used to this kind of success. Mexican families that had been in the valley for two or three generations, working the land, had managed to send their kids to school, and they in turn had gotten good jobs, or else they came back to the valley to open a machinist's shop or an accountant's office or contract for new construction. More people were moving in. Chico was a hard worker, and they admired his ambition. A quiet man, and he didn't swagger. He talked to everyone in a serious, deferential voice. And he didn't make a big show. His wife and girls were neatly dressed, and they carried on their lives like other folks in the valley. He was an official— They said, "That fellow is serious. Does his job. You can depend on him." He did little favors for people, and they remembered it. And though he never spoke of friends in the legislature and in the county, they sensed that he was coming up in the world. He knew people. He knew what was going on in the valley and the county seat. And they admired him for that. If a man came up in the world because of his own efforts, well, he deserved his luck. And if all his people were as hard-working and diligent as he was, why, they'd make it, too. Only they hoped people like him weren't getting too much power, because maybe that wouldn't be a good thing for the future.

Chico knew that his time in the sun would be brief. The next election, his friend would probably be out of a job, and he would be, too. But if he worked hard, maybe he could move on to higher ground. He had many irons in the fire. He was trying for a state job with predator control, which meant going out to shoot coyotes and mountain lions. Once he got in there, he might be able to stay in. And he was trying to work a deal in town to go partners with the sheriff to buy a warehouse. But what he really wanted was land. Now that more people were moving into the valley, the land could be divided up for lots and sold for far more than as orchard or grazing land. Land was his stake in the future.

He was in this frame of mind when something caught his attention. He discovered that Goat Man paid no taxes. Land right there down by the river, some with apples on it, the rest of it going wild, in brush and little thickets. Land somebody could put a decent house on. And how far back did his property go? Who owned that land? He went to the courthouse to find out.

He couldn't find a deed. He couldn't even tell how much of the land belonged, if it did belong, to Goat Man. As far as he could tell from the records, the land had once been part of the Merced ranch, and before that had belonged to a larger parcel. Maybe they'd leased the land sometime in the past when there was still open range and only a handful of people. Could've been just a verbal agreement. Then the ranch had changed hands, and nobody knew that this land had once been part of it. And if the old man had no deed . . . And had never paid any taxes. Maybe he wasn't even a citizen.

The first time he went to see Goat Man, he and the boy were outside the back door not far from the river, cleaning trout, one sizable fish and several smaller ones. A small hound, recognizable in the beagle part of her but open to speculation as to the rest, came from under a bench to sniff at his shoes. The old man and the boy kept silence as they regarded him without surprise or welcome. It was all right with him: he'd come on business.

"I've come about the taxes," he told them.

They looked at him as though he were speaking a foreign language.

"I'm a tax assessor for this county," he told them, though he had no claim to the title, "and you're owing the county some money."

"No," Goat Man told him, after working his mouth into the word. "No taxes here. Never been any."

"You've been getting away with murder," Benevidez told him. "You're going to lose this land if you're not careful . . ."

"I own this land," Goat Man said, with a bewildered frown. "Many years."

"Where's the deed?" Benevidez wanted to know.

Goat Man shook his head. "Paid money and signed a paper."

"You better get that deed, or you're in for trouble." He turned then and walked off. There was no deed, he was convinced of it now. Nothing had been filed in the courthouse. But they'd be getting their tax notices from now on, he'd see to that. Then he'd wait for what would happen next. He wasn't going to push the matter of the deed for the moment. The land had simply fallen out of the last purchase. Back taxes were another and simpler matter. With interest piling up.

How Goat Man looked upon the tax bills that began to come now twice a year it was hard to say, for he spoke to no one about them. Perhaps he regarded them with the same kind of inevitability as the frost that sometimes blighted the apple harvest for the year. For he made barely enough money to survive from one year to the next, and it would have done little good for him to borrow on the land, to create one debt by paying off another. When the notice came that, unless the taxes were paid, the land would be put up for public sale, Benevidez received no response. When the time came, he had his friend pay off the taxes in his stead—it would look better that way. Then he sent Goat Man a notice that he would have to leave the land, it was no longer his.

No response. It was what he might have expected. Now he would have to throw him off—but it would be easy.

One evening after supper near the end of February, he went

with two sheriff's deputies to the hut by the river. The weather had now turned warm after a heavy snow two weeks before. The willows along the river had begun to get the goldish hue they take on just before they leaf out. And there was some grass coming. The apple trees would blossom later on. It was a mild evening.

When the men knocked at the door demanding entrance, Goat Man and the boy were just finishing a supper of rabbit the boy had shot that morning. The old man apparently did not understand what they wanted. He kept waving a paper in front of Benevidez's face, till Chico grabbed it, struck a match, and let it sail around the room. The old man gave a yell and went wild. While the men tried to wrestle his arms to his sides, he knocked over a kerosene lamp that caught a bunch of yellowed newspapers on fire. No one knows exactly what happened after that. Perhaps the men tried to beat out the flames. Perhaps the boy tried to fight off the others and get the old man away. Or perhaps, seeing how things were, the boy fled into the darkness to wait until it was safe to come back. When it was all over, the only facts known for certain were that Goat Man had died in the flames and the boy had disappeared in the confusion.

Some folks were horrified when the story came out. It seemed pretty fishy to them that the old man should have died in the fire when there were three grown men who could have carried him to safety and who had escaped themselves. Benevidez was back of it, they said; he'd paid off those deputies and done the old man in. Maybe they'd knocked the old man out first, started the fire themselves, and left him there. They didn't say such things publicly, because there was no real evidence, but a glow of moral indignation smoldered under the surface for a while. If Benevidez was aware of the rumors, he didn't let on. Such things pass over and, after a time, are forgotten.

Plus the fact that there were enough people around who thought Chico was simply doing his job. Folks who paid their taxes and didn't know why Goat Man should have been an exception. He'd gotten away with murder for years. Maybe it'll put the fear of God into some of those illegal aliens, they said. Teach them to stay where they belong. And though Chico had taken advantage of his position to get that piece of land for his friend (and everybody knew what that meant), well, consider what some politicians were getting away with in the very same moment. No, they really couldn't blame him. So they went about their business, and when Benevidez ran for county assessor during the next election, they voted for him.

As for the boy, no one knew where he'd disappeared. There was no trace of him in the cinders of the blackened hut. Could be he slipped away when the fire broke out, or maybe the men told him to start running if he knew what was good for him. Perhaps he hid somewhere there in the darkness, but if he came back to the hut after the flames had roared inside, he must have known that nothing could have remained alive there. Later, they found the little dog cowering among the empty goat pens. Somehow the goats had gotten loose and were found scattered in various thickets along the river.

But the boy never came back, nor was he gotten rid of all that easily. For a time people kept seeing him. He'd sneak down sometimes under the cover of darkness, they said— set the dogs to barking to announce his presence, and then disappear. Others claimed they had seen him during the day. Chickens turned up missing, or a tool, or a piece of clothing. It was curious, people said. You could feel him come and you knew he was there, with a sensation like you get when the air starts to melt in the sun. But if you set out to look for him, in that same instant you knew you might as well save yourself the trouble. Then sometime later a fellow who had gone off hunting along the river for quail said he saw him sitting on a rock under one of the big cottonwoods with his flute in his hands. He stood waiting for the sound of the notes, but the boy had seen him, and when he tried to approach, there was only the rock by the river and the sensation of recent presence.

For a time the charred remains of the adobe hut where Goat Man and the boy had lived reminded those who thought about it that something they were used to was gone. And they remembered the two who had lived there from one season to the next, taking their sustenance from the thin soil, led by some obscure instinct for survival. And they carried a sense that something had changed, not only in their surroundings but possibly in themselves as well, and that an obscure itch would live with them.

After a time the hut too was gone, and the sheds, and the apple trees were torn out, for they were old and diseased and the fruit was of no commercial value. Benevidez was able to sell the land as two parcels, one for a bar that was going in and the other for a new house going up.

Faces keep changing along the Mimbres, people coming and going, including Benevidez himself, who moved north, closer to the centers of power. The stories about the boy are fewer and far between, but they haven't died out altogether. Perhaps one of these days, someone who has never heard about him, say a young couple walking out at sunset, or a man alone hunting, will chance upon a boy sitting on a rock playing a flute, and will hear a melody they can't exactly remember nor will ever entirely forget. A melody that will call something to mind like an old memory or an unspoken desire. Maybe even without knowing it, the valley is waiting for something like this to happen. And if it does, it will seem so real, it won't matter if it's true or false.